# BUSHWHACKED!

As Jessie bent over her coffee, a far-off shot rang out and the cup was torn from her fingers. Ki reacted instantly. Moving in a blur, he knocked Jessie sideways as another shot exploded from the trees. A thick column of sparks shot upward from the center of the fire as the bullet furrowed into the flame and ash.

Two more shots followed them, sending dirt flying up at their boot heels, as, running in a crouch, they made for the cover of a pair of thick pines. As Ki crept out to circle behind their assailant, Jessie fired three fast shots in the general direction of the gunman. She peeked around the side of the tree to see if they'd had any effect. A shot crashed out, and a thick strip of bark splintered at her cheek . . .

## DON'T MISS THESE
## ALL-ACTION WESTERN SERIES
## FROM THE BERKLEY PUBLISHING GROUP

**THE GUNSMITH by J. R. Roberts**
> Clint Adams was a legend among lawmen, outlaws, and ladies. They called him . . . the Gunsmith.

**LONGARM by Tabor Evans**
> The popular long-running series about U.S. Deputy Marshal Long—his life, his loves, his fight for justice.

**LONE STAR by Wesley Ellis**
> The blazing adventures of Jessica Starbuck and the martial arts master, Ki. Over eight million copies in print.

**SLOCUM by Jake Logan**
> Today's longest-running action western. John Slocum rides a deadly trail of hot blood and cold steel.

**WESLEY ELLIS**

# LONE STAR

## AND THE BELLWETHER KID

**J**

**JOVE BOOKS, NEW YORK**

LONE STAR AND THE BELLWETHER KID

A Jove Book / published by arrangement with
the author

PRINTING HISTORY
Jove edition / September 1993

ISBN: 0-515-11195-3

Jove Books are published by The Berkley Publishing Group,
200 Madison Avenue, New York, New York 10016.
The name "JOVE" and the "J" logo
are trademarks belonging to Jove Publications, Inc.

PRINTED IN THE UNITED STATES OF AMERICA

10  9  8  7  6  5  4  3  2  1

LONE STAR

AND THE
BELLWETHER KID

★

# Chapter 1

It had been a long, hard ride, most of it through the worst weather that Jessie could remember in a long time. It rained for three days. And not that soft Texas rain that smelled of green hay and open spaces, either. This was a hard, cold rain, that fell through the pine and poplars, muddying the trail so badly that in some places the horses had a tough time just lifting their hooves. Great muddy streams gushed downward, splashing over the rocks and trail. But then again, they were in the Sierra Nevadas, and Jessie had never cared for them much.

Ki had been silent for almost a full day as they pushed on. They might have waited out the rain a half-day's ride behind them, or they might have taken the train. But Jessie wanted to finish her business in the Lone Star–Sierra Freight Company and get back to Texas. The freight company represented the last Starbuck holding in Nevada, and she would be glad to be done with it.

Jessie looked over at Ki—the water running down his face in rivulets, his hat surrendering its shape to the water, and his oilskin soaked through. He blinked twice and rubbed his face with a gloved hand.

Jessie knew she was just as sorry a sight. She could feel her clothes wet as a spring well under her oilskin, and her shoulder-length blond hair hanging down beneath the soggy hat. She figured she looked like a drowned rat, though that was impossible. Even soaked through, muddied, and tired, she was every inch and stitch a woman. No doubt, all of the clothes in her saddlebags were soaked through as well.

"Perhaps it would have been wiser to take the train," Ki said, glancing over at Jessie. They were the first words he'd said all day, since they woke in the middle of the storm and ate soggy biscuits for breakfast. She was relieved that there was no malice or anger in his voice.

"What would we be doing now?" he asked, his half-Japanese face arranging itself into a sly smile. "Perhaps eating a rare steak, baked potato and butter, and apple pie in a too warm dining car? And listening to drummers?"

Jessie felt only a slight pang of regret. Yes, steak would have tasted good. Some dry clothes would have been welcome as well. "Yes, I suppose you are right, Ki," she answered, grinning herself now. "Things could be worse. But I suppose I'm tasting some humble pie now."

They rode in silence for a hundred yards, the rain

hissing down through the trees from the steel-gray sky. It would be dark soon, and they would have to find a place to make camp.

A small river ran down in front of them. It couldn't have been more than three or four feet wide, but Ki, as was his habit, spurred his horse forward to take the river first. As the horse eased its way into the icy water, it suddenly stumbled, letting out a openmouthed whinny of complaint and falling nearly to its cinch before recovering. Jessie urged her horse on, taking the stream closer to the trees.

By the time Jessie reached Ki, he was already down in the mud, examining the hoof. "How bad?" she asked, reining up alongside him.

"Not bad," Ki said, releasing the hoof.

Jessie breathed a small sigh of relief at the news.

"But cannot ride," Ki added. "Make it worse in the mud."

Jessie sighed again, but this time not with relief. Without saying another word, she pulled her foot from the stirrup, and reached down to help Ki up.

He slid gracefully up behind her, then handed over the reins, which she gave a turn to around the pommel. It wasn't the first time they'd shared a horse. She only wished that the last time had been *the last time*. Doubling up on her chestnut would slow them down even more. And she wanted to get out of the rain as soon as possible. Next time they would take the train.

• • •

It was after nine in the evening by the time Jessie and Ki made Wygone. The light in the distance held some hope for Jessie. She was still thinking of steak and apple pie. But as they reached the town's main street, she saw that her rising spirits had been in vain. The town wasn't any more than a crude collection of shacks and canvas lean-tos that extended down the trail for maybe seventy-five yards. Only two buildings had a second story. One was a saloon/hotel, the other a livery stable.

Jessie had seen towns like it before. Planted between a railroad and a mine, the town served the few dozen miners up in the hills surrounding it, but more importantly it was a stopover for the Washoe wagons that brought the ore down for processing. When the rails reached the mine directly, the town would cease to exist.

Jessie and Ki came down off the horse they were riding, then hitched both horses to the post in front of the saloon. With any luck they'd be able to find a couple of plates of ham and eggs and some dry beds.

They pushed through the batwings, entering a saloon that wasn't much warmer than the outside. Though it was considerably dryer, and for this Jessie was grateful. A small knot of men were hunched over talking at the far end of the bar. There were six of them, and Jessie recognized five immediately as miners and local businessmen. The sixth was wearing a brown broadcloth coat, a silver brocade vest, and a clean shirt. The shirt alone was enough to make him stand out.

Jessie and Ki stood just inside the door for a long time, sizing the situation up. Finally, Jessie removed her hat and began stripping out of her heavy oilskin. Ki looked for a heartbeat longer, listening to the clink of pans catching water from the leaking roof, then joined her.

The row of heads at the other end of the bar turned as if they were attached to a single string. It wasn't until she reached the bar, and its mirrored wall behind, that Jessie saw what they were looking at. The rain had soaked her through so thoroughly that the material of her tight-fitting canvas britches and worn blue shirt clung to her tightly enough that nothing was left to the imagination. Jessie could feel her nipples hardening under the material, then all at once saw them in the mirror. They poked out proudly against the soaking fabric of the shirt.

Jessie did her best to hide her awkwardness and embarrassment, nodding to the group of men. A few offered slight nods back to her. All of them continued to stare.

"You seem to have attracted attention," Ki said, sidling up alongside her.

"You'd think they'd never seen a woman before," Jessie answered in a whisper.

"Probably they have not seen so much of a woman in public before," Ki said. Then he added, "For free."

The bartender, a short fat man, hurried over. "Ma'am . . . ," he began, but before he could finish, Jessie heard a commotion coming from the group, then saw the man in the brown coat rushing over, the green cloth from a faro layout held in both hands.

"Will this do?" he asked the bartender, draping Jessie in the cloth.

" 'Spose it'll have to, Mr. Sturgis," the bartender said. "What'll it be, miss?"

"Whiskey," Jessie said. She needed something to take the chill off.

Ki shook his head when the bartender turned to him.

The bardog was busy getting Jessie's drink when the gentleman who'd rescued her said, "I'm afraid you have me at a decided disadvantage, ma'am," touching a polite finger to his low-crowned hat. He had a smooth, eastern voice.

"Starbuck," Jessie said, accepting the liquor as she slid a coin across the counter. "Jessie Starbuck. And this is Ki."

The man nodded toward Ki, then said, "Byron Sturgis, at your service. Starbuck, I know that name."

Jessie drank down the whiskey for an answer.

"Starbuck, Starbuck, it will come to me," Sturgis mused. "A newspaperman never forgets."

Jessie put the glass down on the bar and nodded to the waiting bartender for another. "Is that what you are, a newspaperman?"

"And proudly so," came the answer, along with a slight, though very dramatic, bow. "A poor scribe who chronicles the sad comings and goings of the weary world. A watcher of human drama. Daily—or at least weekly—chronicler of incomplete history. In short, a reporter."

6

Jessie took a sip from the second drink. She could feeling herself warming up. Perhaps even the gambling table's cloth was of help. "Thank you, Mr . . ."

"Sturgis," the reporter said.

"Mr. Sturgis. Now, if you don't mind, I must see the livery about the horses."

"Done and done!" Sturgis shouted. Then to the bardog, "Have the boy fix up Miss Starbuck's horses, immediately."

The bartender gave the reporter a look that said if he hadn't been spending money all night, then he'd have fixed *him* up. Immediately. Rather, he just nodded and went to the back room, presumably to wake a dozing lad and lead the horses to the livery.

Jessie could feel Ki cringing beside her. She had known Ki all her life and damn well knew when someone didn't suit him. And this Sturgis jasper sure didn't suit him. But in his usual style, Ki kept silent.

"Now, Miss Starbuck," Sturgis began. "What brings you out on a night like this?"

Jessie sipped some more at her drink and said, "Business I'm not at liberty to discuss, Mr. Sturgis."

"A mysterious woman out in the storm accompanied by a yet even more mysterious gentleman of the Far East. Miss Starbuck, am I more or less in the vicinity of a story?" Sturgis asked.

Despite herself, Jessie couldn't help but smile. Sturgis was, if nothing, amusing. "Hardly," she answered. "We have business in Carson City. I'm afraid you'd find it rather dull."

Sturgis, undaunted, smiled and said, "Business concerning a beautiful woman could never be dull. Now, could it?"

Jessie drained the last of her drink and looked around for the bardog. But he hadn't returned.

"I'll see to the horses, Jessie," Ki said. And then he was gone through the batwings as he slipped back into his oilskin.

A few of the men at the other end of the bar began to drift off with the sure knowledge that Sturgis would not be coming back to buy them liquor anytime soon. From where Jessie stood, she saw that this was not an altogether disagreeable proposition. Free whiskey was small payment indeed for having to listen to a newspaperman.

"And may I ask what your business is in Wygone?" Jessie said, noting that a young lady was now moving behind the bar. She wore a bright red dress and perhaps just a touch too much powder on her face. Her reddish-brown hair was piled up high on her head. And her cinched dress revealed a rather shapely figure. Jessie, like all women, was not beyond noticing such things.

Sturgis inhaled loudly, which probably meant he was getting ready to talk for a long time. Jessie signaled the barmaid by holding up her glass. If Sturgis was going to talk for any length, she'd need some fortification. Already, she could tell, listening to this man would prove thirsty work.

"A story, Miss Starbuck," he began. "A story

brings me to Wygone. Perhaps the greatest story, more or less, I've yet penned. A yarn of death and tragedy, and the rugged individualism that made this Western wasteland a rich mine of myth and inspiration for our Eastern readers."

Jessie raised her glass, noting that the last of her money on the bar had vanished with the filling of it. "Mr. Sturgis, do you always speak like that?"

"Like what?"

"Never mind. Please, continue if you must."

He wasted no time. "As I was saying, I'm hot on the trail of a story. I hesitate to mention it, but I can see you are a woman of substance, high ideals, and character in addition to great beauty. So, I believe my trust is well placed in you. Miss Starbuck, have you ever heard of the Bellwether Kid?"

"I can't say that I have," Jessie said. Then she took another drink. The story was threatening to be even longer than she had dreaded.

"You haven't?" Sturgis asked, somewhat surprised. "Well, no matter. He has more or less been written about in the Eastern papers. The Bellwether Kid is perhaps, more or less, the best gun to ever ride, to shoot, to break a girl's heart. A killer he is. Bounty hunter. Drygulcher. Regulator, if you will. A hired gun. He rides alone. A sole man riding through the wilderness on a trail of blood and vengeance. A knight of the modern era in a strange and primitive land."

"More or less," Jessie said, unable to help herself. She had listened to what he'd said. And as

9

far as she was concerned, this Bellwether character sounded like a dozen or more guns she'd run into. Probably more reputation than anything else. And more than anything else, a reputation fueled by men like Sturgis, who celebrated their pathetic exploits, making back-shooting cowards into heroes.

"Yes, more or less, indeed," Sturgis agreed, unaware of the slight. "And my sources tell me he is due to pass this way soon."

Jessie took her drink and turned, noticing that the other men had completely vanished. They'd either retreated to a back-room poker game or turned to bed. "Is there a room, two rooms, available?" Jessie asked, turning back to the woman behind the bar.

She nodded grimly. "Cost you two dollar a night," she said. "Breakfast included. That'd be ham steak and coffee. Biscuits. But you got to fight them others, wagon drivers, for them."

Jessie took even closer notice of the woman now. She was a fair-skinned girl, not more than twenty-two or twenty-three, perhaps a little plump, but with a sweet smile, a smile that was strained considerably by Sturgis.

"Excellent accommodations!" Sturgis broke in. "Highly recommended. You won't find better."

It was just then that Ki came back through the door. The rain outside had not let up, and he was soaked through again. "The bartender owns the livery," he said. "Horses are in for the night. Might take a few days for that fetlock to heal."

"We can decide in the morning," Jessie said, all at once feeling bone tired from the ride, the rain, the whiskey, and Sturgis's talk. "I'd like to go to my room now."

The young woman strode out from the end of the bar as the bartender came back. "This lady would like a room," she said to the older man.

A small smile broke the man's face, and he ushered Jessie back. "How about your friend there?" he asked, nodding back toward Ki.

"I think I will have something to drink," Ki called. "I'll be along. Soon."

Jessie followed the bartender through the back door and up a flight of rickety stairs. There were five rooms altogether. Under one, the light shone through and the sound of drunken laughter could be heard.

"Drivers. Washoe wagon drivers," the bartender said. "They're a rough bunch, but shouldn't bother you none."

Inside, the bartender lit a small lamp, illuminating a windowless room that wasn't much larger than the small bed that sat in its middle. A basin of water rested near the door, next to a slop bucket. It was the most beautiful room Jessie had ever seen.

"I'll have the boy bring up your things," the bartender said.

"Thank you," Jessie answered, then fell right into bed, soaking clothes and all. She pulled the faro layout tight around her, not bothering with a blanket, and was asleep so fast she barely had time to shut her eyes.

11

• • •

Downstairs, in the bar, Ki felt the soft eyes of the barmaid pressing against him, which he figured was a whole lot better than that Sturgis fellow bending his ear. The newspaperman had in fact left shortly after Jessie turned in for the night.

"I have some French brandy," she said. "From France."

"I do not often drink," Ki said. "But . . ."

"For medicinal purposes," the young woman finished and reached under the bar for the bottle. "For French medicinal purposes."

"Exactly," Ki said, not at all sure what she meant.

She poured two glasses and handed one to Ki.

The brandy tasted of peaches and old wood, not at all disageeable. He finished it in a gulp, then set the glass down carefully on the bar as he felt the liquor warm him.

"Would you like another?" the woman asked. Her glass, too, had been drained.

"What if your boss returns?" Ki inquired. "Would you not be in trouble?"

"Uncle Cyrus?" she asked. "If he hasn't come back by now, he's probably not coming back. All the paying customers have either left or bedded down for the night."

"Very well then, but I must pay," Ki said, producing a dollar from the small leather sack that hung on his waist.

"Very well then," the woman said. "Call me Sarah."

"Sarah is pretty name," Ki said. "My name is Ki."

"Like what you put into a lock, like that key?" she asked.

"No, not like that key," Ki answered. "But it is too long a story."

"You two ain't married or anything, are you?" she asked as she poured more brandy into their glasses.

"No, we are not married," Ki said, and took up his glass.

By way of answer, she poured more brandy into her glass and said, "That's nice."

"Why is that nice?" Ki answered. But he already knew.

The girl blushed. "Well, just that drinking French medicinal liquor with a married man and all."

"And?" Ki asked, teasingly.

Her face changed to a deeper shade of red, and she turned her eyes from Ki's, dropping them to the floor. "Nothing," she finally said. "Except it would be scandalous."

Ki felt himself smile. "It would?" Ki asked, feigning surprise.

"Sure would," she said, suddenly regaining composure. "But I got to close up for the night." Then she was out from behind the bar, turning off lamps and swinging closed the doors behind the batwings.

When the room was dark, except for a single light by the back room, she approached Ki. "Would you help me with something, Mr. Ki?"

Ki nodded, then followed her to the back room. He was only mildly surprised to see a bed, a night table, and a small mirror in the far corner, back away from the barrels of whiskey, boxes of cigars, and shelves of cards and poker chips.

"This is my room," Sarah said. "Uncle Cyrus got another room, over at the livery."

"I see," Ki answered. "What is it, exactly, I can help you with?"

In the dim light of the room, she blushed again. Her eyes sank downward. "It ain't exactly help. It's more like an opinion," she said.

"Yes."

Then her eyes came back up and she blurted out, "You think I'm pretty, Mr. Ki?"

"Yes, very."

"I mean them wagon drivers, they say I'm pretty, but a belly full of liquor and a ewe gets looking good to them. Sometimes I don't know."

Ki doubted this. He had never met a woman who did not know exactly how pretty she was. But he played along and said, "Yes, you are very pretty."

"I mean for a girl that ain't Chinese and all."

"I am half-Japanese," he answered. "And yes, for any girl, you are very pretty."

"I like my hair," she said, reaching behind her head to loosen the bun. "I've always liked my hair."

Ki watched as she shook her head slightly, bringing great cascading lengths of her lustrous hair falling downward below her shoulders.

When she was finished shaking her hair free, she said, "Mr. Ki, would you mind if I kissed you?"

Ki went to her then, smiling slightly. She fell into his arms, and he bent his head toward her upturned lips. He could feel her quivering slightly in his arms, feel her heart going a mile a minute like a locomotive, but not from fear.

His lips touched hers and then parted. For a long time their tongues did a little dance in the hot wetness of their sealed mouths. She pushed closer into him, her hands exploring the firm muscles of his back.

And he let his hands wander down, from the smooth material that stretched along her shapely waist, toward her firm bottom.

Suddenly she broke away. "Oh, Mr. Ki, I just don't know what's coming over me," she said, breathless.

"Did you not like it?" he asked.

As answer, she began undoing the buttons that ran up and down the front of her dress. Her fingers worked slowly, her eyes fastened on the task. When she had undone all of the buttons, down to her waist, she undid the ribbon that cinched her middle, hunched her shoulders slightly and the dress fell around her buttoned shoes.

Next came her undergarments, which she abandoned with equal ease. In the soft light, her pale skin seemed to glow, taking on the hues of the lamp's flame as it flickered ever so slightly in the chimney.

She was smiling slightly now. It wasn't much

of a smile, but it managed to be knowing and shy and lustful, all at once. "Am I still pretty?" she asked Ki, her voice no more than a whisper.

"Oh, yes," he managed, his voice gone suddenly thick in his throat. "Yes, you are very pretty."

She took a step forward, coming out of the clothing that had gathered about her ankles, and still smiling. When she reached Ki, she began playing with the buttons that fastened his loose-fitting shirt. "But, Mr. Ki, you're still dressed. I think I can solve that problem."

As she began undoing his buttons, Ki reached out a tentative hand and brushed his fingertips across her breast. She shivered with excitement, and her nipple hardened against his touch.

Reaching out his other hand, he took the other firm breast in his hand. It fit exactly into his palm, and he felt the nipple harden as he lifted its warm weight.

"Oh, Mr. Ki," she moaned.

Careful not to touch any other part of her, he continued to gently play with her nipples, slowly rolling them between his fingers, teasing them until Sarah began moaning more and more.

Eyes closed, she leaned toward him, as she managed to unfasten the last button of his still-soaking shirt.

Ki took a step back and shrugged off the garment, revealing his well-muscled chest.

Sarah opened her eyes and took in the sight. "Oh, you are a handsome man," she purred, then brought up her hands to massage Ki's firm chest and stomach muscles.

16

He took her in his arms again, one hand still gently toying with the hardened nipple. Then he felt her knees begin to give out. She sank down, her lips falling away from his as she continued to kiss him. Her lips glided smoothly over his neck, then down, down, down, across his nearly hairless chest and farther down still, until they reached his washboard stomach.

It wasn't until she was fully kneeling before him that she released her lips from his flesh. Then, looking up, eyes filled with mischief, she began unbuttoning his pants.

With the release of the last button, Ki's manhood sprung forth, fully engorged.

Like a cat, she nuzzled into it, placing it first in the warm nest between her cheek and shoulder, then lifting her head slowly, so that she could stroke it with one hand. "Oh, Ki," she moaned, her fingertips playing along the hard shaft. "Oh, you are so . . . so . . . much."

Leaning back slightly on her heels, she lifted her head and ran her lips down the length of the solid shaft. When she reached the base and the soft gathering of midnight black hair, she tilted her head back more, protruded her tongue, and began licking him. Slowly, slowly, she worked her way back up the shaft, until she reached the tip.

Bringing both hands around Ki, she held him firmly and drew the tip into her mouth. For a long time she paused there, just the tip of his manhood between her full, wet lips. Then, inch by inch, she drew him in entirely. When her lips reached the base and her nose tickled from the hair, she slowly withdrew with a tilt of her head.

When he was almost completely out of her, his shaft glistening in the light and just the very tip once again remaining between her lips, she paused. Very slowly she began working her tongue in slow, lazy circles around the tip.

She took him into her again then, swallowing him in a single gulp, letting her tongue run from the tip to the base. When she withdrew again, it was all the way.

"This is fun, isn't it?" she asked, a giggle in her voice, her face glowing. "Oh, do you still think I'm pretty?"

"Oh, yes," Ki answered, wanting to take her then, right then and there.

"Do you think I have a pretty bosom, Mr. Ki?" she asked, then rose slightly, letting his swollen, glistening member rest between her two warm breasts.

"Yes."

"Does this feel good?" she asked, bringing her breasts together, trapping his manhood between them in the soft, warm folds of her flesh.

"Oh, yes," Ki answered as she slowly began to massage her breasts.

He could feel the heat pouring off of her as she began to squeeze him hard between the soft mounds of flesh and rock her entire body back and forth.

Ki threw back his head, letting out a soft moan. But before it was entirely out of his mouth, she released his shaft from its tender imprisonment and held it gently in one hand, palm up.

Slowly, she went back, gently pulling him toward her. Ki was only too happy to oblige. As she sat all the way back, she opened her legs wide, revealing her amber-colored mound of hair, glistening. Glistening, when she hadn't even been out in the rain that night.

Very slowly, she guided him into her, raising her backside just a little off the floor as she teased the tip of his shaft against the moist lips. Then, slowly, slowly, he entered her.

Ki paused, his entire shaft inside, feeling the wet warmth wash over him. She raised her backside again, and he withdrew, pulling himself almost all the way out before stopping.

"Oh, you are a tease, Ki," she purred, as her arms came up to grip him at the shoulders.

When he sank back into her, she pulled gently, and her lips parted in an openmouthed smile.

Little by little Ki built up the speed. And with each thrust, she rose to meet him, until finally they were rattling the boards beneath her.

They reached their moment together—Sarah scrunching down her eyes, her forehead beaded with sweat, and Ki straining as he came to his final release.

Even after he had finished, he left himself buried deep in her warmth. Holding her, he could feel the last quivering trembles of excitement race through her body.

Finally, she opened her eyes and, looking straight into his, said, "Oh, Ki, that was just . . . just about as good as anything gets."

Ki stroked a strand of her hair back into place and was about to say something, but then he heard the scream. And to his horror, it was a scream he recognized as Jessie's.

★

# Chapter 2

Ki burst out of the back room, already fastening the pants around his waist. From the floor above he heard Jessie cry out again.

The rain had stopped, tapering off into a mist that left the rough-hewn outside stairs to the upper level slick. Barefoot, Ki took the stairs three at a time. A razor-sharp *shuriken* throwing star was already in his fist by the time he gained the second-floor landing.

At the top of the stairs, he paused only long enough to see the open door. Then there were more footsteps, and a figure vanished into the room.

Ki, raising the *shuriken*, followed suit, moving like a shadow that slid noiselessly against the wall. Inside, the room was dark. Two figures fought, as a third, Jessie, sat up in bed, holding a peach wood–grip revolver trained on both of them.

"Cad, scoundrel, ruffian, begone," cried

Sturgis's familiar voice. "Quit this young lady's premises immediately. Do you hear me? Immediately, or I shall be forced, nay obligated as a gentleman, to beat you within a wit of your life."

Only Sturgis could talk so much during a fight. Then the other man's hand came up, connecting a solid blow to Sturgis's chest, and the newspaperman flew by Ki and tumbled out the opened door. He landed hard on his backside, which seemed to shut his mouth.

Ki raced past the downed reporter and into the room. But before he could throw a kick or use the *shuriken*, Jessie said, "Now, you just hold it right there!"

Even in the shadows, Ki saw the man's hands go up as the revolver's barrel flashed in the darkness and its hammer clicked back above the brass-cased round.

"That you, Ki?" Jessie asked.

"Yes. Are you hurt, Jessie?"

"Don't think so," she said. "Not so I can feel it, anyway," she said, then struck a match on the floor with one hand and touched the flame to a lamp's wick.

Standing against the wall, hands raised high, was one of the wagon drivers. His suspenders were down around his legs, his fly unbuttoned. "I just came in here, an accident like," he moaned.

"It wasn't an accident, not with what you were trying," Jessie said. Then to Ki, "He would have almost got away with it, if I hadn't fallen asleep dressed."

Ki was about to say something, but the moaning from just outside the door stopped him.

"You better see to Mr. Sturgis there," Jessie said. "I think I can handle this one. He isn't much."

Ki walked back out through the door. There, leaning against the railing, legs sprawled out in front of him, was Sturgis.

"You hurt?" Ki asked.

The question seemed to revive the reporter some. "Hurt? My good man, I have tangled with the Devil himself," Sturgis began. "I have been laid low and mean by a common brawler, a ruffian of dubious pedigree and parentage. I have looked the bloodthirsty killer in the twin abysses he calls eyes and seen death itself . . ."

But before Sturgis could finish, Ki called back in to Jessie, "He's fine. Still talking."

" 'Cause a him I got drunk," the wagon driver said. "Man's got to drink when listening to that kinda talk. Goes on an' on like. Never heard nothing like it."

Cyrus rushed up then, closely followed by Sarah, who had had the presence of mind to change into a nightgown and robe before following Ki up the stairs.

"What in the name of anybody is going on here?" Cyrus asked, stripped down to a pair of long underwear.

"Man broke into Miss Starbuck's room," Ki answered. "Tried to—"

"No need to go into details," Cyrus hastily interrupted. Then added in a whisper, "Least not in front of Sarah here."

The girl just smiled sweetly and said, "Thank you, Uncle Cyrus."

"A pox, a double pox upon your villainous head," Sturgis suddenly shouted. He had managed to come to his feet and was propped up in the door, steadying himself with both hands. "I call you murderer, fiend, despicable scoundrel. I shall deal with you with words. Assassinate you in the press. Oh, do not mistake my skill with fisticuffs with my skill with the pen," he threatened. "I shall pummel you into a bloody, sobbing heap with words. Render you senseless and unable to defend the blows I'll rain down upon your lowly brow at the point of my mighty pen . . ."

"Lady," the driver said, voice pleading. "If you ain't gonna shoot me, then at least shoot him."

Sturgis was about to say something more, but Cyrus silenced him. "What you want to do about this, Miss Starbuck?" he asked.

"A trial, by twelve true and honest men," Sturgis answered for her. "A trial, then a hanging. A hanging is the only proper punishment for such a coward and fiend. A swing on the end of sturdy hemp is what he deserves. Nothing less would satisfy this lady's nearly lost honor."

"What I would like," Jessie began, and with her first words silenced the gathering, "what I'd like truly, is to go back to sleep."

Before the reporter could say another word, Cyrus had closed the door to Jessie's room and was herding the entire crowd back down the stairs. "Darling, I think you best spend the night with me," he said to Sarah when they were at the foot of the stairs. "I expect that more than one of those drivers is drunk."

"Yes, Uncle," she replied sweetly. But as they reached the foot of the stairs and left Ki, she turned slyly and gave him a wink. It was a wink full of promise and not a little naughty passion.

The next morning, Ki walked into the saloon and saw the table set up for breakfast. The drivers sat in a corner table, quiet, as Sarah served them helpings of eggs and ham steaks.

A moment later Jessie was at Ki's side. The drivers, all of them, including the one that had attacked Jessie, bowed their heads, each one suddenly intent on his meal.

Outside, the sun was shining and the mud already drying into cracked earth. The air smelled fresh, the scent of pine in it. No doubt, it would be a good day for traveling.

"Did you sleep well, Jessie?" Ki asked, as they took a seat at the front of the saloon.

"Better, after all the commotion," she answered.

A second later, Sarah was bringing out cups of coffee, eggs, biscuits, and ham steaks. Once again, she gave Ki that lustful wink. It was a gesture that did not go unnoticed by Jessie, though she decided not to comment on it. Ki's personal affairs were his personal affairs. Long ago she had made the decision not to comment on them. Though she did allow herself the slightest smile. A gesture that did not go unnoticed by Ki.

They were halfway through their meal when Sturgis entered the saloon. He was wearing a black suit, a clean white shirt, and a low-crowned hat. Except for the color, it was nearly identical to the outfit he'd worn the day before.

"If we're quiet, perhaps he will walk past us," Ki said. "There is always that chance."

"No such luck," Jessie answered. And as usual she was right. Sturgis made a beeline for their table, pausing only long enough at the drivers' table to snort.

"Miss Starbuck," he said, bowing elaborately. "My good fellow Ki. How does the morn find you, much rested and refreshed I would hope?"

"Yes," Jessie answered, taking a bite of her ham.

Ki only nodded.

Without asking, Sturgis sat down, but not before removing his hat and making a little show of removing an imaginary speck of dust from it.

"And how do you feel, Mr. Sturgis?" Jessie asked. "It appeared last night that you received the worst of it."

The reporter winced a little at the slight, but let it pass. "One can never receive the worst of it while defending a young lady's honor. Posterior, if I may elaborate, does indeed feel rather tender."

Jessie suppressed a smile, and let the comment pass.

"I have of course remembered the name Starbuck," Sturgis said. "A small miracle I did not recall it sooner."

"Of course," Jessie answered.

Sturgis put on a large smile. "Yes, indeed. Are

you not *the* Jessica Starbuck of the Starbuck fortune in Texas? Tell me I am mistaken and I will purchase this fine morning repast."

"The breakfast is included with the rooms," Ki answered.

"Of course, of course it is," Sturgis said, pressing onward. "But I am not wrong, am I?"

Jessie finished chewing and swallowed, taking her time with both. "You are not wrong, Mr. Sturgis," she said with an attitude of surrender.

"By crippled swifts and blind editors, I knew I was correct," Sturgis answered, slamming a hand dramatically on the table. "I would have bet my byline on it."

"Now that you've discovered me, Mr. Sturgis, I can only hope that you will do me the honor of respecting our privacy," Jessie said. "It would be the gentlemanly thing to do."

"Oh, make no mistake, Miss Starbuck, I am a gentleman," Sturgis replied with a sincere tone.

"Thank you, Mr.—" Jessie began.

"But I am a newspaperman first," he answered. "And a gentleman, alas, second."

Ki watched as Jessie seemed to sink deeper into her chair with the revelation of this bit of news.

Sturgis seemed not to notice. Pulling a small notepad from his pocket and the nub of a pencil, he asked, "Now, if you'll be so kind as to tell me your business in Carson City. It was Carson City, wasn't it?"

Something unspoken passed between Ki and Jessie. Together they rose, pushing out from the table in unison. "I would like to, Mr. Sturgis,"

27

Jessie said, "but we've already spent a good deal of sunlight. We must—"

The reporter only smiled. "I'm afraid I've taken the liberty of checking on the condition of Ki's horse," he said with a shake of his head. "The animal is still, I'm sorry to say, not fit for the ride. Another two days at least. And the coach doesn't arrive for another four full hours. So I'm afraid, Miss Starbuck, you have time enough."

Jessie, sensing she was trapped, and oddly in debt to the reporter, sat back down. Ki followed suit, occupying himself with his breakfast, which had suddenly, since the arrival of Sturgis, become tasteless.

Jessie, true to her obligation, told Sturgis everything. She relayed in the dullest possible manner how she planned to sell the freight company to a partner and then go back to Texas. She made a point of mentioning that she could not wait to leave for her home state.

Halfway through the story, which lasted no more than five minutes, Sturgis stopped writing. When she was completely through, he closed the notebook and rested the pencil atop it. "Dry commerce, Miss Starbuck," he said. "You have told me a tale that would lull a bookkeeper to slumber. Surely you have had some adventure on your trip. Some tidbit or wild men or animals or bandits. Something that would gratify my readers."

"Sorry to disappoint you, Mr. Sturgis," she said, satisfied that nothing she had said would see print.

"Oh, a newspaperman is never disappointed,"

he said. "Perhaps his editors, on rare occasions his readers, and every day his mother. But a newspaperman, never."

"Well then, I'm sorry to disappoint your editors and readership," she said, again rising.

Ki rose, too, more bored than annoyed.

"But wait," Sturgis cried, coming out of his chair. "Allow me at least . . ."

However, his cries, if they did not exactly fall on deaf ears, were ignored. By the time his voice died in mid-sentence, Jessie and Ki were already out the door, the batwings swinging.

"We should try to continue by stage," Ki said.

Jessie, who had never been fond of the Concord stages, agreed. The ride would be a tough one, two days at least. But it would get them out of town and moving toward Carson City. And at that point neither of them cared much how it came about, just as long as they made some progress toward their unfinished business.

★

# Chapter 3

The Fargo man was a little plump fellow who seemed as if he'd be easily flustered. A schedule for coaches across the territory hung on the wall behind the high desk that fronted the office in the small building. It was the schedule that he referred to when he spoke to Jessie and Ki.

"Got a stage arriving today at eleven sharp," he said, squinting at the schedule. "Maybe on time. If it's late, won't be but an hour late. You understand, if it's an hour late arriving here, it'll be an hour late arriving at the next stop."

"That's fine," Jessie said.

But the little man went right on ahead. "Hour late at Soda Springs, makes it an hour late leaving, you understand?"

"Yes, we understand," Jessie said, reaching into her pocket for some money.

"Three more stops, three days riding to Carson City," the clerk said. "After Soda Springs you got three more stops. Hour late in each. Now, I'm assuming it won't find any more trouble 'long the way. Can't say that it will, mind you, but I can't say that it won't."

"Yes, I would imagine that," Jessie said, counting out the twenty-five-dollar fare for her and Ki.

"Know what that means, don't you, missy?" he answered, pushing his tin spectacles far down on his nose.

"What?"

"Means you get into Carson City an hour late," he said, with no little triumph. "Hour late, at least. That is, if the stage don't run into any more trouble 'long the way. Don't ask me if it will. Ask me and I can't tell you. You understand that, don't you?"

"I understand that," Jessie replied, pushing the money across the worn counter, toward the little man. "I understand that completely."

"Just didn't want you blaming me," the little man said, still not taking the money. "Wells Fargo and Company just travels the roads, can't rightly lay claim to their condition. Coach is an hour late, can't blame the company. Not at all. Especially not after I told you such."

"Please, just two tickets," Jessie insisted.

"Might not even be an hour late," the clerk said. "Might be half hour late. Depending on weather and the team, might not be late at all. Might be two hours late. Can't properly tell. Not with weather."

"It doesn't matter, at all," Jessie groaned.

The clerk pushed his spectacles back up his

nose. "Now, don't get all uppity with me, missy," he shot back. "Ain't my fault, not at all, if the stage is an hour late."

Even after that, it still took some doing and patience on Jessie's part, but she finally managed to buy a ticket. It was, she mused, a wonder that they sold any tickets at all.

After the ticket was officially stamped with the seal of the Fargo Company, they walked back to the livery to see about selling the horses.

Jessie had traded horses before she was giving second looks to boys, and been around horse traders since before she could talk properly. Old Alex Starbuck had trained her well in the shrewd ways of the business of buying and selling. She not only knew what to look for in horseflesh when she was buying, but how to make a decent bay or claybank gelding look like a prize.

The way Jessie saw it just then, she could probably get as much, maybe a little more, than they had paid for the horses by selling them to Cyrus. The old man could take some time in letting Ki's animal heal up, then sell it off to a drummer passing through or retrain the both of them for a wagon team. Both animals were strong enough. But the main thing was not to let him know they were leaving in just a few hours on the stage. Because the very second a seller's got to sell, then the buyer's going to walk away better for the bargain.

They found Cyrus in the barn, sitting on a stall gate, watching a local boy clean out the opposite stall. Jessie could tell he was just wasting

32

time, smelling horse patties and listening to the flies buzz.

"Morning again, Miss Starbuck," Cyrus said in greeting. "Come to see how your animal's getting along?"

"Thinking about it," Jessie answered, and unhitched the stall where her horse was lodged.

Cyrus watched the little show Jessie put on; the way she checked the hooves, and the water, and the hay.

"Fine animal you got there, Miss Starbuck," Cyrus said, as Jessie came easing out of the stall and locked the gate.

"Ki tells me she's one of the best he's ridden," Jessie answered.

Cyrus cocked an eyebrow, but said nothing.

"And lately, I've been thinking that maybe I need something more suited to the country," she said. "And something more suited to me. More of a lady's horse, you understand."

Cyrus cocked another eyebrow. "Now, you wouldn't be thinking about trading, maybe, would you?"

"Maybe," Jessie said, coming down to where he sat. "Maybe just been thinking about it."

"Both?"

"Maybe," Jessie answered, with a smile that gave nothing away.

"Vance! Boy! You go back to the saloon, fetch me a bottle," Cyrus called to the boy. "Something smooth, something for sipping."

The boy dropped the pitchfork and ran back to the saloon.

"Now, you wouldn't mind if I partook a little, would you?" Cyrus asked. "Ain't too early, I suppose. Early enough for some horse trading, it's early enough for a drink. Perhaps you would like to join me, Miss Starbuck."

Jessie smiled again. It was a ritual as old as horses, she supposed. Horse trading and sipping whiskey were inseparable.

"And your friend there," Cyrus said, acknowledging Ki for the first time. "Perhaps he'd like a little something?"

"Perhaps," Jessie said.

Ki began to smile. It wasn't the first time he'd watched Jessie get down to serious business horse trading. It wouldn't be the last. The entire affair was much like the tea ceremony of his ancestors' country, he thought. Each participant had a role to play, and very seldom did they break away from their proscribed roles. Wherever you travelcd, it was the same.

The boy, Vance, came back in running and clutching a corked pint bottle in one hand. But right on his heels, moving at a quick walk, was Sturgis.

Vance ran up to Cyrus and handed him the bottle. The older man took a drink, then handed the bottle to Jessie before greeting Sturgis.

Jessie raised the bottle to her lips, and was about to take a sip, when Sturgis said, "Heard about your leave-taking, Miss Starbuck. Fargo coach, excellent method of transportation. Don't travel any other way myself, unless of course a railroad is handy. Next to the rails, I wouldn't transport myself east or west, north or south, by any other means. Highly suggested for a woman of your station in life. When money is no object, why not travel by the most modern conveniences?"

Cyrus's immediate reaction was a slow, foxy smile that was on the surface nothing but cordial, though it showed clearly enough the face of a man who'd just filled an inside straight.

Jessie could barely keep from spitting out the liquor in a jolt of anger.

It took more than two hours and a considerable amount of back and forth, but Jessie eventually received almost a fair price for the two horses. By then it was nearly time for the stage to pull in.

Walking out of the livery into the late morning sun, Jessie once again saw Sturgis. He was leaning against a wall of the saloon, looking west down the main street.

As Jessie and Ki walked by on the way to the Fargo office, Sturgis turned slightly and said, "That's him."

Jessie paused, then said, "That's who, Mr. Sturgis?"

And then the newspaperman did the most incredible thing. He didn't talk. Rather, he inclined his head with a nod, toward the far end of the street.

Jessie and Ki's eyes followed the nod. And there, riding a white gelding and sitting on top of a Mexican saddle inlaid with silver, was a lanky man done up in black.

The sight froze Jessie in her tracks.

The lone rider was coming down the middle of the street, a wide-brimmed black Stetson pulled low over his eyes, one hand resting on the ivory-grip handle of a shining .44.

As he came closer, Sturgis said, "It's the Bellwether Kid."

And Jessie saw that he wasn't much more than a boy. He looked like he was done up for some fancy-dress party.

The gunfighter came to a halt in front of the saloon, slid down off the saddle and hitched his horse. He didn't look like any hired gun Jessie had ever seen. For one thing, he was dressed too prettied up. The other thing Jessie noticed was his eyes. They weren't the dead, dull eyes of a killer. Rather, they were the clear, wide-open eyes of a boy.

"Ma'am, Mr. Sturgis," the gunfighter said as he passed, then pushed through the batwings.

"The Bellwether Kid," Sturgis repeated with no little awe in his voice. "Did you note, Miss Starbuck, the manner in which the people stopped and stared at his coming. The hooves of his death-white mount seemed to beat a slow tattoo of doom down the dusty street, his approach marked by silence and fear. The heavens seemed to pause in their busy orbits."

"More likely shock," Ki answered. "The way he's dressed, people were more shocked than anything."

"Around his waist a belt of hand-tooled leather," Sturgis continued undaunted. "Inlaid with gleaming silver dollars. A dollar, they say, for every man he's bettered at the draw. A dollar for every lonely grave he's filled. Life in the frontier is cheap, is it not?"

"Not as cheap as talk," Ki mumbled to himself.

"He is the grim reaper in human form," Sturgis finished. "A death's head without the smile, is what they say. A heartbreaker and life taker. A man who makes his own rules."

"Is that what they say, Mr. Sturgis?" Jessie asked, only slightly amused.

"Indeed they do," the reporter answered. He was visibly awed, in a particularly dramatic way. "Oh, indeed they do. Now, if you'll excuse me, I must speak to him. Find what brings him to this part of the country. Perhaps, even, who will be his next quarry. Ruthless rustlers? Murderous gunmen hired by a wealthy cattle baron? The greedy-eyed manager of a mining company? Surely no ordinary villain could bring him so far from the liquor and ladies he holds so dearly and well. It must be some bloody business of the most urgent variety. Don't you think?"

Jessie shrugged for an answer and continued on with Ki toward the Fargo office. If Sturgis wanted to waste his time with some dress-up gunslinger, it wasn't any of her affair. None at all. And besides, the coach would be in at any moment.

They were only a few steps down the boards when they heard the harsh laughter of the wagon drivers. The laughter came through the saloon doors in a whooping chorus, and someone yelled, nearly strangled by mirth, "Now git a lookee at that gitup!"

The Bellwether Kid had arrived. No doubt about it.

★

# Chapter 4

Jessie saw the Fargo man pacing outside his office. He would take two or three steps, turn, then retrace his truncated path, turn, then check his watch before continuing forward. He did this at least a half dozen times as Jessie and Ki approached.

Finally he turned to Jessie and Ki and said, "Told you, didn't I? Didn't I say, clear as day, that the stage would be late? Hour, maybe two hours, late I told you."

"Yes, you told us," Jessie said.

"Then why are you bothering me?" the clerk said. "Why? I can't make 'er come any quicker. The company don't expect me to have a hand in anything that takes place outside of town. Can't expect me to. And neither should you. Now, you got no call being upset. None at all. 'Cause I told you. Plain as day."

"We're not upset," Jessie answered.

"I will get the things," Ki said, then turned and

headed back for the saloon.

"If you're not upset, then what you doing here?" the clerk whined with an air of authority. "Tell me that then, what you doing here when there ain't no coach?"

"Waiting," Jessie answered. "We're waiting for the coach."

This seemed to take the little clerk back some. He pushed his glasses back up to his eyes, looking up and down the street, checked his large Elgin pocket watch again, then finally said, "Ain't no law against that, I suppose. You ain't got a choice but to wait, no matter how damned late it is, I suppose."

"Thank you," Jessie replied and sat on the long bench that ran across the front of the office.

"Now what are you doing?" the clerk snapped, turning on her suddenly.

"I'm sitting down to wait," Jessie said.

The clerk seemed to deflate again. "Most people don't wait for the coach here," he said. "Most wait over at the saloon. I'm in the habit of walking over and announcing the coach. For mail and such. Can't remember the last time someone waited on the bench."

Briefly Jessie thought about following Ki back to the saloon. But the idea of facing Sturgis and the Bellwether Kid put her off the idea. She'd rather wait with the nervouse clerk than a newspaperman who ran at the mouth. "Well, this will give you something to talk about then," Jessie said. "Next time someone takes the coach out of town."

Jessie was just settling back to wait when she heard the commotion coming from down the street. It was enough of a racket to cause the nervous clerk to freeze in his tracks.

Someone was yelling in the saloon, then two someones were yelling, and a third joined the argument. Jessie came up off the bench to get a better look. The saloon was maybe fifty yards down the street, but she could see clearly enough.

"At it again," the clerk said. "Right on schedule, them damned wagon drivers."

Jessie watched as one of the drivers, the one who'd assaulted her the night before, came backing out of the saloon. Next came the Bellwether Kid, followed by a dozen or so loafers and other drivers. It was Sturgis who brought up the rear.

The first wagon driver stomped to the middle of the street. He was grinning and joking. A couple of his compatriots stood on the boards, calling encouragement to him. Nobody was calling encouragement to the Bellwether Kid; he looked alternately as grim as death and scared to death.

When the gunfighter was halfway to the middle of the street, the driver pulled an ancient Navy Colt from his belt and fired, raising a bit of dirt at the Kid's feet. The gunfighter startled, but kept coming.

Then the two men stood there facing each other. Suddenly the scene grew still. One of the drivers on the boards said something and went for his gun, no doubt to torment the youthful gunfighter, but quick as a flash, Ki was through the batwings, his hand gripping the man across the collar hard

41

enough to prevent him from going for his gun.

Jessie heard the clerk vanish inside, the door slamming behind him. For a second she, too, thought of retreating, but decided there was no danger. The gunfighter and driver were so close, not more than then yards apart, they'd have been hard pressed to miss each other.

The driver had replaced the gun in his belt and was staring steadily at the gunfighter. They both stood there for what seemed like a long time; then, as if by some predetermined signal, they both drew.

It looked to Jessie as if the Kid were bested on the draw, his fancy Colt barely out of the holster by the time the driver was firing. But all at once there was a shot that actually sounded like two shots, and the driver spun, a red hole blossoming on his chest.

The Kid fired again, and this time the shot went wild, smashing through the window of the saloon. When he fired a third time, it took a chunk out of the wood on a building across the street, and Jessie was beginning to think that maybe she should have taken cover inside the Fargo office.

The Kid raised his gun again as Jessie began to retreat, but it was too late. The shot sang out, and she felt a sharp pain bite through the back of her jeans. She sprang through the door as the gunslinger emptied his gun.

The wagon driver didn't die, right then and there. It took a good two hours. When the time finally came, he said, "Aw shit." A second later he was gone.

Jessie saw this, of course, because she was stretched out in the doc's office, lying flat on her stomach with a bandage covering her wound.

"Nothing I could do for him," the doctor said, covering the dead man with a sheet. "Bullet hit an artery. He just sort of leaked to death."

The doctor was young, not more than thirty, and of a muscular build. His shaggy blond hair hung down over his collarless shirt. Even as he worked on the dying man, Jessie admired his build.

"I suppose I should attend to you, Miss Starbuck," he said, turning toward Jessie.

"It's not serious, really," she replied, wiggling slightly. And in truth, it wasn't that serious. Barely hurt at all. What smarted worse was the way she was stretched out on the table, pants pulled down around her knees. It was damned humiliating.

"Now, just let me be the judge of that," he said, then removed the sheet that had covered her wound. A small bandage had been placed over the spot, and a tiny drop of blood leaked through it.

The doctor let out a low whistle as he removed the sheet. It was the kind of whistle that left Jessie wondering if he was admiring her back end or the wound, or both.

"Now, that's not too serious," he said, his voice soft and low as he examined the area. "Really, not much more than a burn. Won't even take a stitch."

"That's what I thought," Jessie said.

"Just let me apply some salve to it," the doctor said, and withdrew to his cabinet.

A moment later he was rubbing warming salve across the area. Perhaps he was rubbing it a little too much across the area, his soft hands making slow circles over the smooth skin of Jessie's back end.

She didn't want to complain. His gentle touch was causing her to wiggle, just ever so slightly, with pleasure.

A moment later he was applying a bandage, wrapping it around her leg and up slightly over the wound. And she was pretty certain that if one of the beefy drivers had been hit in the same area, his hand wouldn't have strayed quite so far up, to brush against her silken fleece. Nor would the driver have rubbed, pressing ever so gently, toward him.

"That will do it for now," he said, his voice slightly choked. "Though you're going to have to stay off it for a few days."

"Stay off it, how?" Jessie asked.

"No riding," the doctor answered, wiping his hands on a clean cloth. "No unnecessary activity. You don't want to inflame it."

"But I have to be on that coach," Jessie replied, easing off the table and fixing up her trousers.

The doctor turned, smiling only slightly. "Miss Starbuck, that coach left an hour ago. Even if you could have been on it, I'd have recommended you not be. Not at least for two days."

Then there was a slight knock at the door, and the doctor called, "Enter." Jessie hoped she wasn't blushing as the door came open slowly. When Ki appeared, she let out a small sigh of relief.

"I have brought another pair of pants for Miss Starbuck," he said, addressing the doctor.

"Ki, where I was shot didn't affect my hearing," she said, and took the fresh pants.

"Will she be all right, Doctor?" he asked.

"And it didn't hurt my ability to talk either," she snapped, as she eased her foot out of the old trousers and into the new ones.

"I think that pretty much answers your question," the doctor replied, smiling.

"Come on, Ki, let's get out of here," she said, pulling up her pants and easing back down into her boots. "Doctor, how much do I owe?"

For a second the young doctor seemed taken back. "Didn't you know?" he asked. "The bill was settled before I treated you. Before you were carried into the office."

Jessie's face must have betrayed her ignorance of this. Now, who would pay her bill?

"The man who shot you, that Bellwether Kid, paid for you," the doctor said.

★

# Chapter 5

Jessie was resting, lying on her stomach across the bed, when she heard a timid knock on the door.

She knew that it wasn't a secret she was staying up at the saloon's hotel. Nor was it a secret she'd been shot in the butt.

The knock came again.

"No visitors," she called.

The person knocked once more, then the door opened. Jessie, turning her head slightly to the side, saw it was the so-called Bellwether Kid. He was holding a handful of wilted flowers.

"Now, what do you want?" she mumbled.

The boy seemed a little shy. And it occurred to her she'd never heard of a shy gunslinger, much less seen one. All the professional gunmen she'd had the misfortune to meet up with had been loud, bragging types. Loud and bragging or dead.

"Came to see how you was doing, Miss Starbuck," he said at last.

"Well, you've seen, now get," Jessie stated.

"Brought you these, Miss Starbuck," the young man said, extending the flowers cautiously. "Figured they might brighten up the room some."

"Well, you'll just excuse me if I don't get up," Jessie answered. Even flowers could not improve her mood at this point. Damn it, she wanted to get out of town, like an hour ago, and this bumbling gunfighter had shot her just bad enough to make that impossible.

The boy blushed again, noticing for the first time that Jessie's legs were bare from the knees down. Above the knees she was covered by a faded quilt. "I'll just leave them here, by the door like," he said, then began to back out of the room.

"That's what you do, then," Jessie said.

But the boy wasn't quite through the door when he bumped square into Sturgis, who was coming into the room. "I see you two have made acquaintances, excellent, excellent," he bubbled. "I knew the kid here was a gentleman at heart. Knew it all along, as I know the night follows day. Morning follows night . . ."

"And you follow him out of my room, please," Jessie said.

"Ah, but I've heard the report," Sturgis said with some triumph. "You'll recover, good as new. But the question remains. It lingers in the mind like a seed in the freshly turned earth. Waiting, waiting, waiting to bloom."

"And what question would that be?" Jessie asked.

"What, after your trying adventure, do you have

to say to readers back East?" Sturgis blurted out.

"Mr. Sturgis?" Jessie asked, reaching a hand down under the bed.

The newspaperman leaned forward, ready to record whatever tidbit of information Jessie might see fit to impart to him. "Yes, my dear Miss Starbuck," he said.

When Jessie brought her hand back out from under the bed, she was holding her pistol, the one with the peach-wood grips. "Mr. Sturgis, if you and the Bellwether Kid, or whatever he calls himself, don't leave my room immediately, I'll shoot both of you," she said, voice flat.

"Yes, yes, of course, we quite understand," came the reporter's reply as he began backing through the door, the gunfighter along with him. "Quite right, you need your rest. If I may just ask one favor. A small one."

"What would that be?"

Sturgis, emboldened by Jessie's willingness to entertain a question, came forward a step. "May I see the wound itself?" he said. "For the edification of our readers."

By way of answer, Jessie clicked the hammer back, the sound causing both Sturgis and the gunfighter to vanish out the door.

"So it looks as if you two will be staying, for a few days anyway," Sarah said to Ki.

"Yes, it would appear so," Ki replied.

They were standing in the storeroom at the back of the saloon. From beyond the thin wall came the voices of drinking men and a few laughing women. Cyrus was behind the bar, serving up his liquor.

"I'm s'pose to be doing inventory," Sarah said, displaying for Ki the writing tablet and pencil she held. "I don't imagine you'd have any notion to help me."

Ki shrugged. It didn't matter. With Jessie shot, he was stuck in town the same as her.

"Good then," Sarah said. "Now, you hold the ladder while I climb up and see what's on that top shelf."

Ki grabbed the ladder firmly as Sarah moved between his arms and began climbing, pencil and tablet in one hand. As she made her way up the ladder, Ki took note of her fine shape and the way her dress bunched and curved in all the right places. But then, as she came up so that her feet were eye-level to Ki, he noticed she wasn't wearing any stockings or shoes.

"I just find them so, so confining at times," she whispered, taking notice of his gaze. She knew that she had a well-turned ankle and had no intention of not showing it off for the mysterious visitor.

"What else do you find confining?" Ki asked, letting one hand come off the ladder to caress her ankle and calf.

"I would just suggest that you look for yourself," she giggled.

And Ki did. Lifting the worn calico of her dress, he looked up and saw that she must have found all undergarments confining.

Sarah giggled again and spread her legs slightly.

Ki could hear the commotion from the next room—saloon noises, but so close that at any minute anyone could have walked through the door and discovered them. Somehow, though, that fact only made what they were doing all the more exciting.

Ki bent his head and kissed Sarah's firm leg, letting his lips linger for a long time against the smooth white skin. He could feel her stiffen under his touch, but she made no move to turn away, or climb farther up the ladder and out of reach.

"Oh, Ki, you are a charmer," she purred, and brought both feet down a step, so that Ki was now positioned between her body and the crude ladder.

He kissed her again, this time farther up the legs, allowing his lips to trace a small, gentle design against her flesh.

She purred again and came down a step.

When he kissed her the third time, his lips met with the sweat-sweet flesh of her firm thigh. He lingered there for a long time, head hidden under the material of her dress. Then, slowly, slowly and gently, he poked his tongue out and let just the tip play along the inside of first one thigh, then the other.

She let out another long purr of satisfaction and trembled under his tongue's touch. Ki could imagine her above him, knuckles white on the ladder, her eyes closed, and her lips—those full, sensual lips—parted just slightly.

Ki ran his tongue up the inside of her thigh, higher and higher. He craned his neck until just

50

the tip of his tongue ran along the soft, silken fur he found.

Sarah let out a moan as her body trembled. But Ki did not linger too long in her secret spot. Rather, he brought his tongue slowly, slowly down the opposite leg. "Oh, Ki, Ki, Ki," she sighed, chanting his name as she lowered herself slightly on the ladder.

Again, he ran his tongue up her leg, alternately licking and kissing the smooth, quivering flesh. Little by little he let his tongue and lips playfully make their way higher, until once again he reached the silken mound. Taking a soft tuft of hair between his lips, he pulled gently, then released it, teasing her in the most delicious way.

She trembled again, then quivering, tried to lower herself to him. But he was too quick. "Oh, please, don't," she said. "I want you. I want you now!"

Ki kissed his way quickly up her leg and found the mound again. This time he pulled the silken hair lightly, released it, then let his tongue play gently within the moist crevice he found there. He probed slightly at first, then deeper and deeper, burying his tongue in her tangy wetness.

Her legs were opened as wide as the ladder allowed, just wide enough so that her soft thighs touched his ears, the hair of his head tickling her lightly on the inside of her legs.

Deeper and deeper he probed with his tongue, then very gently he raised a hand. Letting his fingertips barely touch the silken hair, he applied pressure, ever so slightly, to her mound.

She let out another moan and brought a hand down from the ladder, trapping his head next to her. Then slowly, slowly he began to move his hand in small circles, caressing that most sensitive part of a woman.

Her hand tensed, gripping him harder by the hair, as she strained not to make a noise against the pleasure she felt. For a cry of pleasure now would surely bring her uncle Cyrus, and worse, perhaps even some patrons, rushing through the door of the back room.

Ki kept working at it until he could feel the moisture running down his chin. He sank his tongue deep inside her, probing her most intimate and sensitive places, until she leaned forward, pinning him to the ladder.

And then her moment came. Ki redoubled his efforts, working his tongue faster and faster, then slipping a finger down so that it, too, was inside her.

She trembled and shook, gasping with pleasure, until finally, he felt the sweet release ebb from her body. But he did not stop immediately; rather he released her slowly, little by little, until she let out one final purr of satisfaction.

When it was done, she stayed on the ladder, barely hanging with one hand, a private, soft smile across her face. Ki worked his way out from under her dress, then gently reached up and lifted her down. As she descended to the floor, she wrapped her arms about his neck and held tightly. Then, turning, she raised her lips to his and kissed him deeply and passionately.

"Oh, that was so-o-o nice," she cooed, slowly breaking the kiss. "Now let me do something for you."

Ki leaned back against the ladder as she slowly went to her knees in front of him. A small, playful smile went across her lips as she unfastened the front of his pants and reached inside to pull out his already erect member.

For a long time she just held him in her hand, petting his shaft gently and running her fingertips up and down its length. Then, very slowly and gently, she lowered her head and began licking him. Starting at the base, she worked her way farther and farther up, her sly tongue teasing and testing the hardened shaft from underside to top and right on up to the very tip.

Ki could feel her warm breath on his manhood as he leaned back. When she had his member completely wet, she moved her mouth away and grabbed him gently. The palm of her hand was smooth as she began to massage him. First she went slowly, then faster and faster, as she let her fingers play up and down, like some musical instrument.

Several times she licked at her palm, making it wet. Then, once again, when she grew bored, she went back to work on him with her tongue, letting it trip and fly over the hard flesh.

When her tongue reached the top of his member, she took him into her mouth, lowering her head over him in one smooth, long stroke. She let his manhood rest there for a long time, then looked up at him with large eyes and began moving her head back.

Nearly the full length of Ki's shaft slid from her mouth, but she caught the tip, just as it as it was between her lips, and let her tongue dance along it before taking its full length back into her. Finally, she began working him in long, slow strokes.

Her head bobbed steadily as the glistening member slid first into her, then out. Again and again, she nearly lost the tip from the grasp of her lips, but each time she caught it just as it was about to slide from her moist grasp.

Ki felt himself tensing, felt the moment upon him, and grabbed her head. He pulled her to him, and he exploded inside her mouth when the full length of his shaft was buried in its warm, wet chamber.

She swallowed and swallowed, accepting all he offered. And when he was finished, she licked at him, cleaning the full length of the shaft before releasing it from her mouth. But even then she held it in her hand for a long time. She held it tenderly as she rose to her feet, then very gently and a bit regretfully, she tucked it back into Ki's trousers and fastened them.

"See, now we've made each other happy, haven't we?" she asked, face glowing.

"Yes, you have made me very happy," Ki said.

"Have I worn you out?" she asked. "I hope I haven't."

"No."

She was about to say something else, her fingertips playing along the side of Ki's arm, when the door burst open, sending a thick slice of light into the room and startling both Ki and Sarah.

For a moment Ki couldn't make out the figure, except that it was large. Very large indeed.

"Damn it, I sure hope you have that inventory done," Cyrus called from the doorway. "Need it right quick."

"Yes, Uncle Cyrus," Sarah answered sweetly. "Ki here was just helping me with it."

"Well then, is it done?" came the response.

"Almost. We're just finishing up now."

★

# Chapter 6

Jessie, walking with a decided limp, made her way down the stairs and into the saloon. She'd be damned and late for dinner if she had to spend another minute in the room. The plate that the girl, Sarah, had sent up was good enough, but soon after she ate it, Jessie had felt the walls of the room closing in. Even half a day in the room was like a prison sentence. And besides that, her butt just didn't hurt all that much anymore.

As she edged her way through the back door of the saloon, she was hit by a cloud of smoke and laughter. The placed was packed, if twenty or so men could be called a tight fit. But Ki was nowhere in sight.

Making her way to the bar, Jessie was well aware of the fact that she was turning heads. But that was nothing new. She'd turned heads from the Pecos to the Canadian border. It was just something she'd learned to live with, though she wondered sometimes if she'd ever learn to live *without* it.

"Good to see you up and about, Miss Starbuck," Cyrus said as he approached behind the bar. He was grinning ear to ear, the way a saloon owner grins when his place is full and liquor is flowing over the bar.

"Whiskey, please," Jessie said, and put down her coins. She hadn't bought much, but hoped that what she had would help her get to sleep. The wound wasn't so much painful as it was downright annoying.

"And whiskey it'll be, Miss Starbuck," Cyrus answered, pouring her a drink. "Must say, you didn't take long to heal. I'd say you're a tad tougher than you look, if you don't mind my saying so."

"This'll help," Jessie said and sipped at the liquor.

Cyrus vanished with a nod and a smile, easing off along the bar to serve more liquor. Jessie turned her back to review the scene. There were a couple of Faro tables, and a chuck-a-luck, but the real action was taking place off in one corner, where a pretty girl was dealing poker to six men. A small crowd had gathered around the table for what Jessie supposed was a table-stakes game, and the object of their attention seemed very definitely to be the Bellwether Kid.

As Jessie watched, the Kid called a bet, then a raise. When it came time to show cards, his two pair lost to three of a kind. The crowd around the table let go with a small laugh. It was the kind of laugh reserved for losers who are also strangers, and happen to be dressed peculiar.

The Kid either didn't seem to notice the laugh or was used to it. If you dressed like a character in a dime novel, Jessie supposed, then you'd probably get used to people laughing at you at poker tables. What he did was to begin counting his chips. But that didn't take long, because there weren't many of them. And Jessie wondered if he was used to losing, as well. Judging from his lack of chips and the tall piles building in front of the other men, Jessie guessed that the boy had been losing for some time.

She was about to wander over to get a closer look at the game when she felt a gentle hand at her elbow. Looking around, she saw that it belonged to Sturgis.

"Good evening, Miss Starbuck," he said, tipping his head forward by way of greeting. "I see you're enjoying yourself watching our young friend play. As skilled at poker as he is with a firearm."

"He doesn't seem to be doing so well right now, does he?" Jessie agreed.

"Well enough," Sturgis replied with a sly wink. "I myself believe he's merely luring them in through clever play. Leading them down the primrose path. Lulling them, as it were, into a state of overconfidence, laziness, and indifferent play. Weaving a trap of fifty-two cards from which even the most clever will not escape."

Jessie took a look at the table. If the Bellwether Kid were lulling the other players into laziness, it was only because after they left the table, they wouldn't have to work for a spell. "I see," she said, finally.

"Poker is a very civilized game, really," Sturgis explained. "A game of manly sensibilities. A trial by fifty-two cards by which one can judge a man's intestinal fortitude."

"I see," Jessie said, just to fill the small hole Sturgis had left in the conversation. That's what people like him did—leave small holes in their small talk.

"A woman of your delicate sensibilities, I wouldn't expect to understand, or rather to fully comprehend, the more subtle aspects of the game."

"I wouldn't expect," Jessie said, still staring at the game.

"Indeed," Sturgis continued with a exclamation of triumph. "Indeed, it is a game that puts a man face-to-face with his opponents. Mixing equal measures of luck, courage, skill, and concentration. And what, may I ask you, is manhood itself, if not those very elements? Like the very elements of nature, fire, water, air, and earth, so it is we judge a man by his luck, courage—"

"She's dealing seconds," Jessie interrupted suddenly, though without surprise, cutting Sturgis off short.

The little man seemed to stammer wordlessly, then turned full toward Jessie. "What?" he asked finally.

"I said the dealer is dealing the third man seconds," Jessie repeated. "She's bringing out cards from the bottom of the deck."

"You mean cheating?" Sturgis asked, surprised. "Surely you cannot possibly be suggesting that the lovely young dealer is manipulating the cards toward a dishonest end?"

"Yes, that's exactly what I mean," Jessie answered flatly. "Watch, he'll turn up three of a kind."

They watched, and a few moments later, the player turned up three of a kind, again beating the Bellwether Kid. The Kid seemed to be the only one at the table who was surprised.

Sturgis's face was filled all at once with a dim horror. "But this is entirely beyond the pale. Entirely," he stammered. "She's cheating!"

Jessie wasn't surprised. But she guessed that the dealer was only cheating the Kid. How else would she be able to keep bringing those cards up from the bottom of the deck in such an obvious fashion? More than likely, everyone at the table knew it, but they'd been winning and weren't about to complain.

"Mr. Sturgis, why don't you go back and write that a house dealer in a Nevada saloon cheated at cards? If you wrote that, how many people would be surprised?"

Sturgis thought about that for a moment before answering. "Few, I would surmise," he said. "But the brazen little minx is cheating so boldly."

"If you can't spot a cheat, you have no business sitting down at any table but for dinner," Jessie added, and turned back.

"Somebody must tell him," Sturgis exclaimed and hurried off through the crowd.

Jessie wandered back toward the bar. No doubt there'd be a lot of shouting and yelling in the next couple of minutes, and she wanted to be as far away from it as possible. What she really wanted was to be in Carson City.

From her vantage point standing at the bar, Jessie watched as Sturgis rushed up to the gunfighter and whispered in his ear. The young man's face first went all bright, then drained completely of color.

Jessie knew that if the Kid had an ounce of sense in him, he'd call the young woman on the deal, catch her cheating. But the Kid didn't even have that much sense. As soon as Sturgis stepped back from the table, the Kid said something. Jessie couldn't be sure what it was, but it got a laugh from those watching and the other players.

"I said you're cheating," the Bellwether Kid screamed. "Cheating and I won't have it."

Then one of the other men said something, and the gunslinger took a poke at him. It wasn't the best punch Jessie had ever seen, but it had enough genuine anger in it to be effective.

The crowd parted, expanding like a blacksmith's bellows, then surged forward to better see the fight. When Jessie could see the poker table again, the man the Bellwether Kid had tried to punch had the dapper gunslinger by the scruff of the neck and was hustling him toward the door. Anger, it appeared, had once again lost out to skill.

A second later the Bellwether Kid was through the batwings, and the entire bar was laughing. Sturgis, walking with a strange dignity, followed the would-be gunfighter out into the night.

The batwings had not even stopped swinging when Cyrus came running out from behind the bar to settle what was left of the commotion. And what was left was mostly laughing at the gunslinger's expense. Cyrus bought the house a round of whiskey, then hurried behind the bar to settle up.

Jessie just stood at the bar, crowded as the men pushed alongside to get their free whiskey, and more than a few were also free with their hands. She was about to leave when she heard the shot. The whole saloon heard the shot and rushed the door, like a pen of hogs when the slop was dumped in the trough.

"Damn! He shot him," someone said.

And then someone else said, "I didn't think he had it in him. Not at all."

Jessie walked slowly over to the door. She couldn't see much, peeking over shoulders, but she could see enough. Out in the narrow street stood the Bellwether Kid. A few yards away lay the dead body of the man that had hustled him out of the saloon. One hand was fastened to his gun; the other clutched the bullet wound in his chest, blood pouring out from between the fingers and blossoming dark down the front of his shirt. He hadn't left a winner after all.

"Someone go fetch the sheriff," Cyrus yelled. "Real quick, now!"

A few moments later, the sheriff, a rail-thin man with a hangdog look, ambled up the street, a ten-gauge scattergun hanging in his right hand. He was one of those slow lawman who made damn sure they were going to shoot the right man if shooting were what was called for, but were not afraid to admit a good-natured mistake two or three times a year.

The sheriff took the Bellwether Kid's pistol, stuffed it down into his own belt, and started talking to him in a low voice. A moment later the doctor showed up, just in time to pronounce the hour late, the crowd morbid, and the man dead.

"Well, that tears it," the sheriff said. "Gonna have to lock you up, least till I figure out what to do."

"I understand," the Kid said mildly.

"Ain't all bad," the sheriff said, leading him back down the darkened street to jail. "Got some cobbler left over from dinner, if you've a mind."

The Kid turned on the sheriff, looking back over his shoulder, and said, "I ain't all that hungry just now. All that blood and all."

The lawman let out a little chuckle. "Damn if you ain't something," he answered. "Shoot down two men in two days, and a little blood puts you off your feed. You are a genuine something, all right."

"Never cared much for blood," the Kid answered by way of explanation. "Thought it should stay inside is all."

"Wonder you eat at all, being in the line of work you're in and all," the lawman said and chuckled again.

"I try, Sheriff, vegetables and all," the young man said. "Momma always thought vegetables were the important part."

"You are a natural wonder," the lawman said, just loud enough for the gawkers and loafers to hear.

# Chapter 7

Jessie was still standing at the bar, her wound comfortably numbed from whiskey, when the doctor walked in. Most of the other patrons had cleared out—back to bunkhouses, mining camps, and whatever other meager accomodations the town offered. There was plenty of room at the bar next to Jessie, and the doc slid right in.

"Well, that's done," the doctor said to Jessie. Then to Cyrus, "Whiskey."

"What's that?" Jessie asked, turning to meet the doc's tired gaze.

"Inquest," he answered. "Figured we could put him in the ground tomorrow. That man that was shot, he don't have no people, so tomorrow's the best time. Man that digs the graves charges more for working Saturday and Sunday. And that fella might be a little ripe by Monday, seeing as the shot ripped up some vitals once it was in him."

Jessie took a small drink from her glass and

asked, "You're in the habit of holding inquests at midnight?"

"No, but I'm not in the habit of burying more than two in two days," came the slow answer. "So I figured to save the town a little."

Cyrus brought the doctor his drink, and he took it in a gulp, set the glass down, and signaled for more.

"Better slow down," Jessie said.

"That was just a warmer," the doc said. "I'm not much of a drinker anymore."

Jessie studied his face for the first time now. There was something delicate in it. Delicate but not feminine. The thin blond hair, the full lips, the long-fingered hands. He didn't look like your typical frontier doctor—a fat drunk with an unsteady hand.

"Tell me, Doctor, just how'd you manage to land yourself here?" Jessie asked finally.

"Good question," he answered, taking another sip. "I'm sorry to say I don't have a good answer. Not a short one, anyway."

"Try me."

He finished his drink, signaled for another, and began with, "Born into prominent Rhode Island family. Not prominent enough to know the name, just rich in war money. Harvard College, Harvard Medical School. Interned in Boston. Internship cut short by an unfortunate love affair."

"Sounds very tragic," Jessie answered. "And romantic."

"It isn't," he said, taking a cautious sip of his whiskey.

"Isn't what, tragic or romantic?"

"Both," came the answer. "Or is that neither? The chief of surgery's son, a friend of mine, fell in love with a waitress from Quincy. Pretty enough girl. An undergraduate, a senator's son, apparently thought so, too. One night, after far too much sherry, they fought a duel on the Commons. All very funny. Four of us, including seconds, and we could barely stand. All in good fun."

"Who was killed?"

The doctor smiled with grim recognition of Jessie's obvious intelligence. "The undergraduate," he said. "Shot through the eye at seventy yards."

"And you took the blame, out of what, friendship?"

He took another cautious sip of the whiskey. "That and the fact it was my pistol," he said. "The plan was for me to abscond in the middle of the night for a short period. The two families would settle it among themselves, and I'd return."

"But that didn't happen."

"No, that didn't happen," the doctor replied. "The two families were more prominent than mine. It must have been decided that I was to bear permanent blame."

"You were right, it's neither tragic nor romantic," Jessie said.

"A little pathetic," the doctor answered. "But I don't believe we've been formally introduced. My name's Seacrest. Lyle Seacrest. Miss Starbuck, is it?"

"Jessie," she replied.

"Well, Miss Jessie Starbuck, how is your wounded posterior?"

"It's felt better, all things considered."

They talked for a long time. The conversation was far ranging, from Boston, to Texas, to Nevada, from horses to medicine, cattle to debutantes. And the more Jessie talked to Dr. Lyle Seacrest, the more she liked him. He was as unexpected a find in the hills of Nevada as a bottle of good tequila, or the Rio Grande for that matter.

It seemed like a few moments, but in fact it was more like a few hours. Soon, Cyrus, stooped and weary from serving up liquor and smiles all night, closed the saloon.

Jessie and Lyle were just walking through the batwings when the lights in the saloon went off. It was then that he turned and kissed her. It was a full-on-the-mouth kiss, and Jessie's first instinct was to back away, but instead she felt her knees going suddenly weak, and a voice in her head reminded her that she'd been trying to imagine what a kiss from the doctor would be like since he'd applied her bandage.

Finally breaking away, the doctor said, "You'll have to pardon me. I have no idea whatsoever why I did that."

"I do," Jessie answered.

"You'll forgive me, then?"

"I know exactly why you did it," she said with a sly smile, and kissed him again.

The second kiss lasted much longer, with Jessie

pressing herself against him and the doctor pulling her forward with a hand at the small of her back. Even through the denim of her trousers, she could feel his hardening manhood. She rubbed against it, moving her body in a slow, circular motion, then very slowly she snaked a hand down and gave his throbbing member a playful squeeze through the material of his pants.

When they broke away again for air, Jessie said, "I don't know how. With my wound . . ."

But Lyle silenced her with a gentle finger to her lips. "Trust me," he whispered with a devilish grin. "I am after all a doctor."

The doctor's office occupied a storefront at the far end of town. His private rooms were in back. Walking through the office in the wee hours of the morning, Jessie felt a certain illicit tingle run through her. It could have been the late hour, or the whiskey she'd consumed, but maybe, just maybe, it was the fact that she was about to play doctor with a real doctor.

Lyle Seacrest had barely closed the door behind him and lit the small table lamp, then Jessie rushed into his arms. To her complete delight, she noticed that the hardened bulge in his trousers had not softened in the least.

"You'll be gentle," she whispered teasingly. "Remember, I'm an injured woman."

Seacrest let go with a small pleasant chuckle and kissed her full on the mouth. "Oh, I'll be gentle, I promise you that," he whispered. "You won't feel a thing."

"Well, I certainly hope I feel *something,*" Jessie purred.

With that, Seacrest began unbuttoning the front of her shirt. He began at the very top button, his fingers working nimbly, then bowed his head to kiss each new inch of flesh he exposed with his adroit efforts.

Jessie leaned her head back and let out a soft moan as he undid the last button, exposing more white flesh and the ivory-colored undergarment beneath her shirt. Then, pulling the shirt off her shoulders, he brought his lips to them to kiss their smooth slopes, first one, then the other.

Kneeling in front of her, Seacrest next helped her off with her boots, as she balanced on his low desk. As he came up again, he unfastened her belt buckle and trousers. The garment slid smoothly down Jessie's slim hips to the floor, and she stepped out of the trousers gracefully and stood in front of the doctor in her scant underthings.

"Oh, you are a beautiful woman," he said, his eyes moving from top to bottom and then up again.

"I'm surprised you didn't notice earlier."

"That was business," he said, his voice gone long and lustful.

Jessie knew he was maybe partly lying. Hadn't his hand brushed her ever so lightly? Hadn't he sent that thrill through her entire body with just one ever-so-slight touch against her secret place? But rather than question him, she merely said, "And this?"

"Strictly pleasure," he answered, with a smile

that was at once serious and playful.

A few moments later she was naked and standing before him. Suddenly Jessie was very conscious of the steady motion of her breasts, rising and falling with each breath she took. She could feel her entire body tingling with excitement at standing before this handsome man naked as a jay. Naked, that is, except for the bandage on her rear. A strange thrill ran through her, being naked to him, offering herself so blatantly to him.

"Now it's your turn," she said, and took a step forward.

He met her step, and they kissed again, his hand coming up this time to toy with her left breast. Very gently he took the nipple in between two fingers and turned slightly, hardening it so it tingled with pleasure.

She wrapped her arms about him, and he dropped his other hand, brushing her silken tuft with just his fingertips, sending a teasing thrill through her.

Moving back slightly, she reached down and began unfastening his pants. Greedily, she reached her hand in to grasp his hardened member in her long fingers. It was larger than she would have supposed, and Jessie had a difficult time bringing it out into the air.

They stood there for a long time, their hands gently exploring each other's bodies. Jessie felt as if caught in some wonderful unhurried dream. Just then, they seemed to have all the time in the world. All the time there was was theirs.

When she began unbuttoning his shirt, she was

again surprised. His build was not one of a man who spent his days in an office treating the sick. His chest was powerful, his arms corded with muscles. She kissed at him greedily, her lips, half-opened, tracing a lazy line down, down, down, to his hard belly.

Jessie was half-kneeling then, still mindful of her wound, as she began to unfasten his pants, all the while toying with the erect shaft, her fingers gently teasing the very tip. As his pants fell to the ground, he stepped out of them, just as she had stepped out of hers a few moments before.

Once again they came together in a passionate kiss, her breasts crushed against his powerful chest, his erect shaft, hot and throbbing, nearly like a living thing against her pale white belly.

Then, all at once, he leaned down, gathered Jessie into his arms, and lifted her as if she were no more than a feather pillow. She raised her mouth to his and kissed him as he carried her to his quarters in the back of the office.

Very gently, as if she were china, he set her down on her side across his narrow bed, careful that her wound was up. Then he stretched out next to her. Face-to-face, they were so close she could feel his breath. Reaching out, his let his fingertips play across her body, tracing intricate patterns, from the hollow of her neck, down between her breasts and across her nipples, and past her belly until he was gently tangled in the golden tuft.

As his hand worked its way down, grazing across her slender thighs, she parted her legs slightly in brazen invitation. Again he brought down his fingers, briefly playing across her forest of silken hair, drawing a low moan from her.

She could feel herself melting toward him, wanting him as she'd never wanted a man before. Reaching down, she let his thick shaft rest against the palm of her hand, fingers tickling its underside as she brought him up to rub the engorged tip against her moist cleft.

"Now, please," she whispered, almost begging. "I want you now."

He smiled then, a sly, lazy smile, and kissed the side of her neck, burying his face in her streaming hair, drinking in her scent as a thirsty man drinks from a full bucket.

She rubbed his shaft harder against her, so that the tip was glistening with her wetness. "Please, now," she moaned.

Seacrest rose slightly, coming up on one knee, then gracefully moved above Jessie until he was behind her. For a moment she felt his slick shaft brush against the backs of her thighs, a hot and solid touch that sent yet another thrill through her.

He kissed her again, this time on the back of her neck, and she moved one leg slightly forward. She let out a slight moan as the tip of his shaft entered her from behind. Then slowly, oh so slowly and gently, he buried himself in her.

For a long time neither of them moved, each savoring the other. And when he finally did begin, it was with slow, patient strokes that filled her completely before retreating.

Soon he was moving faster and faster, his shaft sliding in and out of her as she rubbed back against him. He brought one arm over her and very tenderly began massaging first one nipple and then the other.

He kissed her again on the back of her neck, then let his hand fall until his fingers were again tangled in her secret forest, probing and massaging her most sensitive places as his shaft continued to build momentum.

She arrived quivering and trembling, and she felt him explode within her. Afterward, they lay still for a long time, each listening to the other's breathing return to normal.

"Oh, Doctor, you certainly have a unique bedside manner," she cooed, and grasped his hand in hers.

"And one which I'm afraid would go wholly unappreciated in Boston," he joked, then nibbled on her ear.

"I'm not so sure about that," Jessie said, giggling. "I do believe that the women in Boston would wholly and entirely appreciate you."

"If that's what you believe, then you don't know the women in Boston," he answered. "They appreciate nothing but old names and new clothes."

★

# Chapter 8

Jessie met Ki in the saloon's dining room the next morning. More to the point, she met him at the front door, as he was returning from the livery.

"The horse is nearly healed," he said. His expression gave nothing away. If he noticed that Jessie was walking into the saloon from the front door, and not the back, and that she had that peculiar smile on her face, he did not show it. Long ago, Jessie and Ki had reached a mutual understanding not to mention each other's personal trysts. It was an agreement that suited each one well, and neither saw reason to betray it in word, deed, or even reproachful glance.

"They are not our horses anymore," Jessie said, leading the way through the batwings. Inside it smelled of whiskey and beer, but she could also pick out the smells of breakfast cooking.

"I took the liberty of purchasing them back," Ki answered, following directly behind her. "Unless, of course, you desire to stay in town another week.

That is when the next stage is scheduled. One week."

Jessie knew Ki had done the right thing, particularly after last night with the good—no, great—Dr. Lyle Seacrest. Jessie knew herself well enough to know that she'd have been no good at horse trading after a night of passion.

"What kind of deal did Cyrus give us?" she asked at last, heading for an empty table in the corner. Three other tables were occupied by wagon drivers, shopkeepers and ranchers in early for supplies.

"If you are asking if we came out the better, no, we did not," Ki replied. "Our good Mr. Cyrus does not give away anything."

"How bad a deal did we get then?" she asked, arranging herself, or rather her injured buttocks, into the hard chair. It wasn't that she didn't have faith in Ki's horse trading abilities, it was just that she'd seen men like Cyrus before. They would, as her granddaddy used to say, steal the eyes right out of your head behind your back.

"Not bad, considering . . . ," Ki said flatly. "Ten dollars more for each horse."

Jessie felt herself smile a little more broadly. It was a nothing less than a miracle that Ki had kept the price down to just ten dollars over what Cyrus had paid for them not a day before. "Not bad at all," she said.

Ki did not return her smile. It appeared that her happiness at the deal was premature. "That is in addition to stable fees for the night, and treatment."

"Wait, but they were *his* horses last night," she blurted out. "He's charging us to board his horses?"

"It would appear so," Ki said. "That is in addition to the liniment he used on the leg. We paid fifteen each above what he paid."

When Sarah came over to the table to take their order, Jessie noticed her doting on Ki. So it seemed that Ki, too, had found someone in such a forsaken place. At least the delay in getting to Carson City had not been a total loss. Still, the quicker they got on the trail, the sooner they'd be on their way home to Texas.

Presently, the eggs and steak arrived and Jessie and Ki began eating in silence. Sarah managed to come by the table only three or four times to ask if everything was fine, and maybe another two or three times to refill Jessie's coffee cup. Each time she spoke to Jessie, but offered Ki a wide-eyed stare of infatuation.

As they were just finishing up their breakfast and preparing to head over to the livery and take possession of their horses, Sturgis came back in through the door.

"If we leave now, we can avoid him," Jessie said, and began rising.

But Sturgis made a beeline for their table. He was smiling broadly from ear to ear and walking with a decided spring in his step. "My dear Miss Starbuck," he began and pulled up a seat. "I have wonderful news. They, the powers that be, have cleared the Bellwether Kid of all charges, large and small. He has, in the eyes and ears of the

77

courts and authorities, been rendered innocent of all wrongdoing."

"That's wonderful news, really," Jessie agreed as she continued to stand. Ki was already up, eager to leave.

"Ah, steak," Sturgis said, noticing the meat left on Jessie's plate. "Do you mind?"

"Please, Mr. Sturgis, help yourself," she responded. "We were just leaving."

"Thank you. My sincere and heartfelt appreciation," he said, grabbing her fork and spearing the hunk of meat. "It has been such a hectic day, even at this early hour."

"I'm sure," Jessie mumbled, turning her back as she aimed herself for the door.

"Now, the only question remaining is how to write you into the story. Miss Starbuck, do you have any suggestions that might help this poor scribe find his way in revealing your personality?"

He could not have halted Jessie quicker if he'd impaled her with the fork and not the leftover meat. She stopped dead in her tracks, her back toward the reporter. When she turned, it was with a slow and deliberate motion. "I beg you pardon, Mr. Sturgis, I don't believe I heard you correctly. Did you say that I am to be part of—"

" 'The Bellwether Kid Saga,' " Sturgis finished. "Indeed, a vital part."

"But I'm not a part of it," Jessie complained. "Please, don't feel any obligation to include me in the story."

Sturgis, chewing on the hunk of leftover meat,

said, "Include you? Why, a beautiful woman injured, nay saved, by the Bellwether Kid, that is the stuff that sells magazines. The very stuff. Why, I could not forgive myself, as a journalist, if I did not include you. Nay, my editor would never forgive me if you were absent from the tale."

Jessie exhaled deeply. "What is it you want, Sturgis? How much?"

"Money?" he answered, still chewing. "Are you offering me money?"

"How much?"

"In return for what, exclusion from the tale?" he asked. "Why, there are those who've paid, uh, tried to pay me for the honor—"

"Let's just suppose that I would pay for the honor *not* to be included. Payable in cash."

"One thousand dollars," the journalist answered quickly. "Payable to me, here."

By the way that Sturgis answered, that quick, almost instinctive response, Jessie knew that it was not the first time he'd been paid to keep a story from print. But right now she herself was willing to pay to keep the scribbler from writing anything about her, especially regarding the wounds she'd received and their locale. "Five hundred," she answered. "Take it or leave it."

Sturgis actually seemed to consider this, chewing the last piece of fatty meat slowly as he thought. "I believe I'll leave it," he said at last. "Good day to you then."

"Six hundred," Jessie said.

"I'm sorry, did you say something?" he asked.

Beside her, Jessie could feel Ki tensing. She knew

79

he was itching to dispose of Mr. Sturgis in the most unpleasant manner. And for a second she actually considered having him do something.

"Eight hundred," she tried wearily.

Sturgis opened his eyes slightly, smiled, and shook his head no.

"Listen, you couldn't possibly receive that much for a story," Jessie argued. "A story with me getting shot in the butt couldn't be worth more than fifty dollars or so."

The reporter put the fork down very carefully and looked Jessie right in the eye. "But you miss the point, entirely, Miss Starbuck," he said in a calm voice. "I am a journalist of the highest integrity and moral fiber. What you are asking me to do, even as I think of it, tears at my soul. It pains my spirit. It cheapens the name of good writing, not just for me, but for my fellow scribes. I would not compromise myself for anything less than the stated price."

Jessie had heard enough. She hated Sturgis so much that she'd be damned if she'd give him a cent. "You're nothing but a damned whore," she hissed, leaning in close.

"We're all whores, everyone," he replied smoothly. "It's just that some of us know our price, while, sadly, others do not."

Jessie reached out and slapped him, hard. The blow snapped his head back, knocking his hat onto the floor. Instantly Jessie felt much better. "Write what you damned well please, then," she hissed and walked out of the saloon with Ki behind her.

Outside, Jessie turned to Ki. "He's a new breed of son of a bitch," she said.

"He can make trouble for you, Jessie," Ki answered. "Perhaps it is better to pay and be done with it."

"Not a cent," she said. "Not a damned cent."

They were just approaching the livery when the door burst open and a horse galloped by. The animal looked just like the one Jessie had purchased for the second time, its rider the Bellwether Kid. A moment later another animal followed, a young girl perched on top of it. The fact that the second animal looked like Ki's mount struck both of them as a little more than coincidence.

Jessie and Ki ran, reaching the livery door just in time to nearly collide with Cyrus, who was running out. He was cursing a blue streak, a Winchester repeater clutched in one hand. Narrowly avoiding Jessie, he ran a few more feet, pointed the rifle into the air, and fired off a half dozen shots.

Jessie and Ki stood there waiting for him to return. When he finally did, he said, "Looks like somebody stole your horses, Miss Starbuck."

"My horses?" Jessie asked.

"I believe that your friend here bought them back, not two hours ago," Cyrus said. He wasn't smiling at his good fortune, but close to it.

"My horses?" Jessie asked again, incredulous.

Cyrus moved the rifle from one hand to the other, wiped the back of his neck, and said, "We didn't actually change money, yet. But we shook on it. Ain't that right?"

"He is right," Ki said.

Jessie just stood there, watching the dust settle back down to the street. How could a day that began so well start going so bad? But then again, nothing except the doctor had gone right since before they arrived in town.

"Miss Starbuck, you feeling poorly?" Cyrus asked. His voice sounded almost concerned. "You're looking a mite funny, if you don't mind me saying so."

"I suppose I'm just having a bad day is all," she finally answered. "You ever had a bad day, Cyrus?"

The saloon and livery owner thought on the question. "I suppose I have," he said. "I've had my share of bad, bad days."

Jessie turned back toward him as if looking for some answer. Perhaps she was even waiting for him to say something that would make her feel a little better.

"But I can tell you one thing, Miss Starbuck," he said. "And I know this for sure and certain."

"What would that be?"

"With all the bad luck I've had, added up, it don't hold a candle to the kind of luck you're having," he replied, a tinge of awe in his voice. "I have never, in my life, seen or heard of such downright bad luck."

Jessie was about to say something in answer, but before she could, the sheriff came running up. He was as red as a beet and madder than it seemed possible for any one person to be. Jessie, Ki, and Cyrus turned to face him.

"Sheriff, that Bellwether Kid stole our horses," Jessie said.

"Stole your horses! That sonofabitch stole my daughter!" he screamed.

★

# Chapter 9

It took maybe five or six minutes for a crowd to gather in front of the livery. Loafers, drinkers, shopkeepers, women and men in from the country crowded around the sheriff. After the crowd reached a good size, of ten or twelve, they all began talking at once. In an amazingly short amount of time, the story was repeated and re-repeated, until finally the crowd fell to silence, all eyes turning to the sheriff.

The lawman looked forlornly at the road out of town and said, "That sumbitch. Now what am I gonna tell my wife?"

"What you gonna do, Sheriff?" someone asked. "Call a posse together?"

"Getting late in the day for that, ain't it?" another voice offered.

"After supper, maybe," someone said.

"Tomorrow's better."

"Best to telegraph word out."

"How old was that old gal again?"

"Old enough."

"Old enough for what?"

"Just about anything, I imagine."

"So it weren't like stealing or nothing?"

"No, nothing like that."

Jessie listened to the jabbering, thinking of her lost horses. And the more she thought on them, the madder she got. It wasn't that they were particularly good horses, Lord knows. She'd ridden and owned better by ten times. She'd even paid more for mounts. The thing of it was, she'd already bought the horses twice. And she'd be damned if anyone was going to steal a set of animals she'd already paid for twice.

In all the confusion, Jessie didn't notice Sturgis, who was standing at the back of the crowd. Amazingly, he wasn't saying anything. He just stood there, mute as a statue.

When the sheriff finally turned heel back to his office, Jessie and Ki followed him. Even as she walked down the street, a plan began to take hold in Jessie's mind. Ki walked silently alongside her, not sure of what she'd want to do, but knowing in his heart that she wasn't just going to give up on the horses.

"Now, what in hell you want?" the sheriff asked outside the door to his office.

Jessie approached the sheriff, walking up close enough almost to crowd him. She was angry and didn't much care who she crowded, lawman or not. "First off, I want my horses back," she said.

The sheriff, defiant, said, "Well, that don't look like it's gonna happen any time soon, does it?"

"It'll happen sooner than you think," Jessie replied sharply. "I'm going after them."

Something deep inside, close to the core of the lawman, shifted. His sagging face visibly sagged just a little more. "Miss Starbuck, they say you're a rich lady," he began. "Now, this ain't no business for a rich lady. Why don't you just forget about those horses? Buy two more, buy a ticket for the coach, hire a wagon to take you off to the railhead. There ain't nothing you can do."

"What I'm gonna do is go get those animals back," Jessie said. "Directly."

The sheriff's face unsagged a bit, fear and anger creeping into it. "You go out there, you won't be bringing the horses back," he stated. "You muck around out there, you're just as likely as not to get hurt . . . or worse, get my little girl hurt. Now I know every lawman within thirty miles. I'm gonna send them dodgers, wires, send a few boys riding with letters. I don't want to see you meddling in this. Keep that pretty nose a yours out of my business, understand?"

"It's still a free country, Sheriff," Jessie answered.

The lawman straightened, his eyes gone steely. "That girl gets hurt on account of you, you'll find just how unfree it is."

Jessie made no response. Rather, she turned her back on the sheriff and headed for the livery. She could well understand the sheriff's fears. But she wasn't about to let horses she'd paid for twice get away. Not only that, she'd been met with nothing but bad luck since she hit town. Going after her property was the only way she knew of to break the run of poor luck.

"Are we really going after the horses?" Ki asked when they were nearly to the livery. He didn't need to ask; he already knew the answer. When Jessie made up her mind about something, nothing could change it.

"Damn right, Ki," she answered, staring straight ahead as she walked.

"Might put us behind even more," he said.

"I'll wire ahead to Carson City."

"And we still more or less end up losing money," Ki offered with deference. He knew he wouldn't change her mind; his only object was to offer her some reason.

"Ki, at this particular point I just don't give a damn," Jessie said, stepping into the cool, hay-smelling darkness of the livery.

They lit out at first light. Jessie rode a roan and Ki sat atop a claybank, two geldings that Jessie was sure she'd paid too much for, but once again, she had been unable to haggle a price with Cyrus. Every minute they wasted meant that the two stolen horses were farther away.

As they passed the last buildings that marked the main and only street in the town, the sheriff came trotting up. "You ain't looking to hurt no one, are you, Miss Starbuck?"

Without reining in the horse, Jessie said, "Just get my property back is all. That's all I'm looking to do. You got my word on that."

The lawman, still running, panted, "If you find

them, you tell my little girl to come home. If you would you do that for me, I'd be obliged."

"I'll do it," Jessie said, then spurred her horse forward. Ki spurred his a second later to keep pace, and then they were out of town.

They'd traveled a few miles before Ki spoke. "It is a fool's mission, what we are doing."

"Maybe, but at least we're heading in the right direction," Jessie answered.

Ki could not argue with her logic. Indeed, they were heading in the right direction for Carson City, but he did not know for how much longer. A bad feeling was settling in the pit of his stomach. And then again, perhaps he was just sad to say good-bye to Sarah. She had not come out to see him leave, though she had snuck up to his room and bid him farewell in her own lovely way. Bid him farewell twice, if the truth be told.

By noon, the trail had still not forked off, so Jessie could be fairly sure that they were heading the right way. To leave the main trail would have been foolish; rocks and steep slopes bordered each side. No, the girl and the Bellwether Kid would be riding straight through. Perhaps they were even heading toward Carson City themselves.

They rode the remainder of the day, talking infrequently, but watching the trail for tracks. The trail was not used frequently, and fresh tracks would not be hard to spot. Indeed, by late afternoon, they had seen a pair of fresh tracks, off to the side.

As the sun began to set, Ki said, "Did you notice that Mr. Sturgis was strangely silent?"

Jessie, eyes still fastened to the trail, asked, "When was that?"

"Before we left," Ki replied. "When the people were gathered around the sheriff. Mr. Sturgis did not say a word. He stood there, just watching. He looked rather worried if you ask me."

"Probably worried about losing that Bellwether Kid," Jessie said. "That was his meal ticket. Now he'll have to go and find himself another gunfighter to write about."

"Maybe," Ki answered, then fell back into silence.

That night Jessie and Ki made camp by a small stream. The night was clear and the forest smelled fresh. For a brief moment Jessie thought that she could almost like this part of the country. Then she thought back on all the hard luck it had brought her and reconsidered.

With the fire burning down to embers, and Ki dozing in the bedroll across the way, Jessie let herself drift off to sleep. They would get a fresh start in the morning. The gunfighter and the girl could not have gone far.

Jessie figured it was a little before dawn when she heard the noise. The sound, a snapping of twigs, brought her eyes open and jolted her fully awake in an instant. Looking across at Ki, she saw that he, too, had his eyes open.

Neither said a word, then soundlessly Ki crawled from under his bedroll. Slowly, *shuriken* in hand, he crept back into the darkness of the trees.

Jessie turned, as if in sleep, and brought her pistol into her grasp. The peach wood–handled .38 fit her hand like a glove. If she had to, she'd fire right through her bedroll.

Suddenly there was a burst of rustling from the trees, and a man's howl. It was a high-pitched animal howl, more like a cry. A second later Ki came bursting through the undergrowth, and in his right hand he held onto Byron Sturgis. The newspaperman gripped his right arm in pain, the silvered tips of the *shuriken* peeking out from his fingers and a bloody blossom blooming through his shirtsleeve.

"Found him sneaking around out there," Ki said, depositing Sturgis at the center of their camp.

"Miss Starbuck, I demand a full and satisfactory answer," Sturgis began. "Nay, an immediate answer and apology as to why this ruffian in your employ has injured me, perhaps even mortally, in the middle of the night. Is this not a free country? Cannot a man come and go as he pleases? What is the meaning of this? What good is it to attack a helpless scribe?"

"Can't you just take him back where you found him?" Jessie asked, already growing impatient with the journalist's chatter. "Just take him the hell back."

"Better not," Ki said. "Not just yet. Better to find out what he wants. He followed us."

"I demand immediate medical attention," Sturgis whined. "Immediate medical attention for this painful wound."

"I suppose we can trade you a bandage for

some answers," Jessie offered. "That would be fair, wouldn't it, Mr. Sturgis?"

"Fair indeed," Sturgis said. Then, as if seeing it for the first time, he looked down at his ruined shirt and the thick mass of blood that was appearing. That's when he passed out cold. The man who made his living writing about gun battles and heroics in the West fainted at the sight of his own blood.

★

# Chapter 10

It didn't take long for Sturgis to come around. He awoke from the faint, just as Jessie had known he would, talking. "I cannot thank you two enough" were his first words. "Of course, I would have chosen a more cordial greeting than a knife in the arm. More cordial by far. But all things considered . . ."

"It was not a knife," Ki corrected.

Sturgis paused, but only briefly. "Of course, but that's of little consequence now. Of little or no consequence, I would say. There is but one thing that matters. Tell me if I am mistaken."

Jessie was digging into her saddlebag for bandages and liniment, something to make a poultice for the wound. "What would that be, Mr. Sturgis?" she asked, not turning her head.

"Why finding the Bellwether Kid of course," came the quick reply. "Find him as soon as possible. And with all due haste, I might, and will, add."

"You would not want to lose your best character, is that it?" Ki asked, ripping a section of Sturgis's shirt to reveal the wound. It was a neat incision, as clean as any doctor's scapel.

Sturgis looked at the wound briefly, felt as if he might faint again, and looked away. "Why, of course, there is that aspect," he said. "But there are other, even more important considerations."

"Such as?" Jessie said, coming from the saddlebag, a bandage in one hand and a bottle of linament in the other. With any luck the linament would burn like hell when she applied it.

Sturgis eyed her with deep suspicion, but continued talking. "Why for one thing . . . ," he began, then trailed off. "He needs me. I can't leave that boy out here alone. There is no telling at all what harm may come to him."

"For one thing, he might die like every other gunfighter I've known," Jessie finished, unscrewing the linament's cap. "Dead broke and not famous. Isn't that right, Mr. Sturgis? When that boy dies, you want to be there so you can write all about it. Paint it up pretty for all your Eastern readers."

"Certainly there is that," Sturgis started, "but believe me, there are other things. I must find him quickly."

"This might smart a little," Jessie said, holding the dark brown bottle up. "Be brave."

Sturgis was about to say something else, but then he got a good look at the bottle. "My god, that's horse—"

But before he could finish the sentence, Jessie

93

poured a generous helping over the wound. Sturgis quivered and shook and let out a cry that would have woken the dead. Ki held him tight, only releasing him when Jessie turned the bottle up again, cutting off the stream of thick brown liquid.

It didn't take long for Sturgis to fall into a deep sleep, exhausted from his trek in the woods. When she was certain that he was sound asleep, Jessie turned to Ki, who was thoughtfully feeding the fire. "So?" she asked.

"So," Ki replied.

Jessie added a small twig of her own to the fire and said, "So what do you think?"

"He did not have a horse," Ki said. "That is strange."

"Horse might have run off on him."

"With his bags?"

"It happens."

"I do not like it," Ki said slowly. "A newspaper-man wondering around without a horse or bags, and following us. I do not like it at all."

Jessie snapped a dry branch in half, fed first one half and then the other to the flames. "What do you think, Ki? Do we just leave him here?"

Ki smiled for the first time since bringing Sturgis back into camp. "That would be an idea, and not a bad one."

"There's another town, half a day's ride," Jessie said. "We can leave him there."

"Yes, leave him and forget about him," Ki answered, then rolled over and immediately fell into a deep sleep.

• • •

It was not a pleasant ride the next day. Sturgis awoke talking and didn't stop. They had been on the trail no more than an hour when Jessie turned to him and said, "Can't you just shut that mouth for a minute?"

In truth, Sturgis could shut his mouth for a minute, but not much longer. A little while later he was jabbering on again.

They reached town a little after noon. The town wasn't much more than Wygone, maybe it was even a little less. Carson City was still a couple days' ride.

Jessie fully expected to water and feed the horses, perhaps buy something for her and Ki to eat, then be on their way. But to her surprise, she and Ki ran into the Bellwether Kid and the sheriff's daughter.

"Miss Starbuck, what are you doing here?" the youth asked, eyes wide with surprise.

"For one thing, I came after my horses," Jessie said. "For another, I have a message for the sheriff's daughter. Seems you made off with all three."

"Peg?" the lad stammered. "She's up at the hotel. Getting freshened up. We're leaving on the stage to San Francisco tonight. We plan on getting married."

Jessie was only mildly concerned with both Peg or the youthful gunslinger. The horses were what she was after. "That's real nice," she drawled sarcastically. "If they don't hang you first."

"Hang me? Why'd they want to hang me?" he

asked, actually scared now.

"Horse thieving for one," Jessie replied. "And daughter stealing for another. That Peg, she's the sheriff's daughter, or didn't you know that?"

The boy's face went from scared to a blush. "Oh, I knew that," he said. "That's how we met, when I was locked up. She brought me in some cobbler. Peach cobbler's my favorite, and she just sat and talked with me. I haven't ever met nobody like her. Ever. See, so that's how we met, in jail so to speak."

Jessie wasn't swayed by the romantic tale. She wanted the horses and to leave. "And just how did you meet my horses?" she asked.

The lad went scared again. "They was the first ones we saw," he said. "Peg didn't think it was like stealing them. She figured her daddy would pay after we left."

"She figured wrong," Jessie answered. "Her father wants his daughter back tied to her mama's apron strings and you tied to a length of hemp."

"You mean her daddy didn't pay you for them?"

"Now you're getting the idea."

"Oh, things aren't working out too good, are they?" he moaned. "But I reckon all couples start out having their share of hardships. Ain't that right, Miss Starbuck?"

Jessie couldn't believe it. The Bellwether Kid must surely be genuinely not right in the head. Nobody right in the head could talk the way he talked. "That's right, they have their share of hardships," she agreed. "But having a groom hanged for stealing horses isn't usually one of them."

It took a little while for the lad to think this over, as if he were seriously considering it. Finally he said, "No, I guess it isn't, is it?"

"Just tell me this," she continued. "Where are the horses now?"

"At the livery," the Bellwether Kid offered.

"And neither one is hurt?"

"No, ma'am, I just left 'em."

Jessie thought for a moment. "I'll tell you what then," she said. "I'll take the horses and we won't mention it again. That's about the best deal you'll ever get, and you won't get hanged in the process. How does that suit you?"

"That suits me fine," the youth said. "Except there's this small little problem."

"And what would that be?" Jessie replied, expecting the worst and yet not knowing what the worst could be. She'd already bought the beasts, twice.

"They ain't your horses no more," he said. "I just got done and finished with selling them. Get eighteen dollars apiece for them. Shook with the man and everything."

Jessie was tempted just to shoot the lad then and there. Men that dumb just shouldn't be allowed to live. At least that's the thought that ran through her mind. But then Sturgis came strolling up. He had an anxious look on his face and was excusing himself and the Bellwether Kid all to hell and back, even before he had reached them.

It took Sturgis maybe eight seconds to wrap

his good arm around the lad and steer him off. Jessie watched, standing near the center of the deserted street, as the two made their way back to the saloon. From the looks of it, Sturgis was doing more talking than usual. The youth just kept nodding his head, listening to the reporter as if he were receiving sage advice. Though Jessie knew that what Sturgis was probably offering him was advice on how best to get killed.

Jessie met back up with Ki outside a small cafe across from the livery. Their plan, such as it was, had gone astray. But none of it should have surprised Jessie. There wasn't a whole hell of a lot that didn't go astray the moment she set foot in Nevada.

"So what do you intend?" Ki asked. "To buy the horses back again? To do so would make the third time you've purchased them. Perhaps it would—"

"No, I'm not gonna buy them back again," Jessie snapped. "If somebody don't want me to have them, then the devil take them."

Ki nodded sagely. "Yes, I agree," he said softly. "They must be bad luck."

"Well then, let's just keep riding till we get to Carson City," Jessie said. "Faster we get to Carson, the faster we can turn tail and head home to Texas."

"Yes, I agree," Ki said.

Jessie turned briefly and saw a young woman walking down the street. Neither Jessie nor Ki had to be told who it was; both of them had seen her before, though only briefly. Somehow, Jessie knew, you didn't forget a face that had made off with one of your horses.

As the girl passed, Jessie said, "You would do best to get home. Your daddy's worried about you."

The words brought the girl up dead in her tracks. She stood there frozen for just the briefest moment, then turned very deliberately toward Jessie. "And just what would you claim to know about it?" she asked, defiant as only a young girl can be.

"I know you ran off on my horse and threw yourself in with a gunslinger and a newspaperman," Jessie answered.

"That was *your* horse?" the girl asked. "Then that makes you Jessica Starbuck."

Jessie nodded, then waited for some kind of apology from the woman. But the apology never came.

"Think a rich lady like you could afford a better horse," the girl said, then walked on.

Jessie and Ki watched her go, her heels slamming down angrily on the boards. "Young people today, they lack respect," Ki said at last.

"Respect ain't all that girl's lacking, Ki," Jessie answered. "Seems to me she could use a helping of common sense, too."

Ki nodded wisely at this pronouncement, but said nothing.

A minute later they decided to walk over to the livery and see what they had in the way of horses. Jessie didn't plan on being too particular. She'd ride to Carson City on a spotted, three-legged mule. She'd mount anything, just as long it wasn't one of those jinxed horses.

★

# Chapter 11

Luck was once again against Jessie and Ki. The livery only had three horses for sale. The first two were the ones just bought from the Bellwether Kid, and the third was a swaybacked gelding with split hooves and teeth so worn and black they looked like he'd spent his life chewing rocks and drinking tar.

The livery owner couldn't imagine why Jessie was so set against buying two perfectly fine animals, but promised to acquire two more by morning. There would of course be a slight charge for the trouble.

Jessie, for her part, couldn't help feeling that they might already have been in Carson City if they'd started out walking from Texas.

Ki remained silent, though hardly inscrutable. Bad luck like this was sure not to end with the purchase of two fresh horses. Something bad was lying for them, and he knew it.

Jessie and Ki had no sooner checked into the

hotel and made their way to the saloon, than Sturgis found them. He was standing near the end of the bar, once again watching the Bellwether Kid play poker as if the young gunslinger were playing with his money.

The Kid appeared to be doing better in this game, but appearances, Jessie knew, could be deceiving. After all, he might have just sat down at the table.

"My dear Miss Starbuck," Sturgis said in greeting. "And how is your wound healing?"

Mention of her wound only made it smart more. The ride had developed the slight graze into a point of extreme discomfort. Hoping to ease the pain somewhat, Jessie ordered a whiskey before offering an answer. "It's doing just fine, thank you," she said after the first sip.

"Bad piece of luck, getting shot like that," Sturgis said too loudly. "Oh, what are the odds against a stray bullet finding such an intimate place? I will no doubt ponder that question until my dying day."

Jessie took another sip of her whiskey. "I'm so glad I've been able to give you something to think about, Mr. Sturgis."

The reporter's face changed only slightly, but enough to give Jessie a hint that perhaps there was something pretty nasty lurking beneath that idiot's veneer. "And what new adventures does the boy have?"

"Understand now, I am just a humble scribe," Sturgis began, "but it's my understanding that a pack of outlaws resides not too far from town. Men of the most desperate nature. Murderers. Thieves. Robbers of the armed variety."

"And he's planning to take them on, is he?" Jessie asked. She was more than a little startled.

"Take them on? Why, he intends on bringing them in," Sturgis said. "Dead or alive. Why, just let me give you a peek at the poster relating the details."

Jessie watched as Sturgis pulled a dodger from his coat pocket and slowly unfolded it before handing it over. The wanted dodger was of the variety that the Pinkerton Agency routinely sent out to lawmen. At the top, dead center, was the large Pinkerton eye. Beneath the eye, in neat typeface, were descriptions of three brothers wanted in connection with robbery, murder, and other assorted acts of mayhem. She could see right off that they were hardcases. The Bellwether Kid had about as much chance of going up against one of them as up against a crooked dealer.

"He can't be serious about this," Jessie said, knowing that Sturgis was probably right. The youthful gunhand was serious.

"Serious as death," Sturgis replied. "He plans to take them on. Then he intends to collect the reward and ride into the sunset."

"With the girl, no doubt?"

Sturgis looked a little puzzled. "Girl?"

"The sheriff's daughter, remember her?"

A small smile played across the newspaperman's face. "Why, the girl, of course. The romantic interest, if you will."

"He plans to marry her, or so I've heard."

The reporter's smile widened. "Oh, Miss Starbuck, you are, after all, a romantic. For the first time you've showed your feminine side," he said. "Why, just yesterday, I dispatched my story to our San Francisco offices. And I assure you that my loyal readers will be treated to a full and detailed account of the love affair. But alas, his type is not for marrying. His breed is the lone wolf, destined to make his way alone or—"

"Die in the going, is that it?"

The smile faded quickly, as if Jessie had just ruined the end of a clever joke. "Yes, exactly," Sturgis snapped and walked off.


Jessie awoke to the sound of a creaking board. She did not open her eyes; in the darkened room, that would have done little good. Rather, she reached slowly down and pulled her pistol from its place under the covers.

The boards creaked again. The sound was that of a boot coming down. A cold chill ran up her spine as she realized someone was in the room with her. She could hear his breathing.

Slitting open her eyes, she saw the figure against the whitewashed wall. A tall man, he stood perfectly still. She brought the gun up just slightly under the covers and aimed. She'd shoot through the blanket if need be.

When the figure moved, coming toward her, she thumbed the hammer back. The distinct clicking sounded like thunder in the tiny room. The intruder let out a small gasp, then laughed.

"So you've taken to wearing a firearm to bed, have you?" Dr. Lyle Seacrest said.

Jessie instantly relaxed, thumbing the hammer down. "Doctor, it's the only thing I wear to bed," she quipped.

The doctor approached the bed, crossing the small room in two steps. "Interesting practice, I'd say. Do you get many complaints?"

"Never," Jessie answered.

The doctor struck a match off his thumbnail, studied Jessie's face for a moment, then touched the flame to a lamp. "I have interesting news," he said, sitting on the edge of the bed. "I think you'll find it fascinating."

"I'm sure it can wait for tomorrow," Jessie said, sitting up in bed to expose her full, round breasts to his gaze as she ran a finger up and down the inside of his thigh.

"I'm sure it can, too," he said, then quickly pulled off his boots and reclined full on the bed.

Jessie wasted no time in scrambling out from under the covers. In a flash, she was kneeling between his legs, her large breasts hanging down as she unfastened his belt, then pants. "I really have missed you," she murmured as she reached into his pants.

The doctor lifted his back end and Jessie pulled the trousers down. In a second, they were off, leaving him naked from the waist down.

Jessie studied his already erect member. Then very slowly she knelt to it, catching it between her two breasts. Gently squeezing her twin alabaster orbs together, she began to massage it.

The doctor let out a soft moan as she manipulated her breasts and his shaft, first one way and then the other. Slowly then, she knelt down farther, so that her chin was nearly touching her chest, and caught just the tip of the member in her mouth.

Still massaging his shaft between her two breasts, she slowly, slowly ran her tongue around the very tip. First she made a small, lazy circle, using just the very end of her tongue; then she took more and more of the hardened shaft into her mouth. Soon, the entire shaft was wet and glistening in the lamplight as she continued to massage it between her breasts.

Reaching down with only minor difficulty, the doctor let his fingers play lightly across her firm thigh, until finally he reached her thick patch of hair. Little by little he twined his fingers in her hair, feeling the wetness grow on his fingertips. Then, ever so lightly, he worked his way up and down the entire length of her inviting lips.

Jessie wriggled slightly under the teasing touch, but did not let up her slow, sensual massage of his organ. Rather, she squeezed her full breasts together harder and began moving them up and down the slick shaft.

The doctor let his fingers wander deeper into her. First one, then two, then three. His fingers were long and smooth and knowing. They sought out her most sensitive places, lingering over them for just a moment, before advancing deeper into her.

"Oh, I want you in me," Jessie moaned, releasing her slick breasts. "I want you in me now, please."

The doctor slowly removed his fingers, letting them glide out of her pouting lips. Jessie inched her way up between his legs, pausing only briefly, to give his organ one long, lingering lick before she rose to squat down on her heels.

Reaching down, the doctor held his shaft, pointing it with one hand as Jessie lowered herself. Teasing her, he ran the tip of his member up and down the front of her moist lips, feeling their heat and wetness. Then she was raising herself more, coming up on her legs, then hovering only for an instant above his shaft before slowly lowering herself down.

The tip of his member probed between her lips as Jessie let herself sink onto it. Inch by inch, she savored the feeling as the thick shaft filled her. When she was all the way down, the doctor reached up and held her two breasts firmly, one finger playing across each engorged nipple. Jessie wriggled with pleasure and began raising herself again.

The hard bed made her job easier, her ankles sinking into the thin mattress as she brought herself up off the shaft, so that only the very tip remained inside her. Then, very slowly, she began to lower herself again. Inch by delicious inch, the glistening member vanished inside of her.

When she was once again filled with his member, the doctor removed his hands from her breasts and held her about the hips, helping her balance there briefly before she began once again to rise up.

He was stronger than she would have supposed. Perhaps stronger than she had imagined any doctor being. But as she once again rose up on his shaft, he helped, lifting with both hands.

Jessie leaned forward so that her breasts were inches from his face. The doctor edged himself up as she began once again to settle back down on the shaft. Using only his mouth, he caught the nipple of her right breast between his lips and gently pulled on it.

Reaching back, Jessie found his delicate privates with one hand. First she ran one finger up and down the underside of the shaft, tracing delicate patterns along its slick side as it entered and withdrew from her. Then, taking him in the palm of her hand, she gently squeezed.

The doctor let out a soft moan, bringing himself up off the bed. Jessie rose up, eluding the length of his shaft as he sought the comfort of her warm wetness. As she began to pull up, he released the right nipple and caught the left. As his lips closed securely around her sensitive bud, she felt herself began to spasm and wriggle.

Then, bringing her hand from behind, she grabbed him by the shoulders, her nails digging into his firm flesh and feeling the hard knots of muscle beneath.

Then, suddenly, he was at his point, too. Thrusting upward, he buried himself in her.

Jessie closed her eyes, and every muscle in her body sang and hummed. Again and again, he thrust into her, each deep probe releasing wave after wave of pleasure. Finally, when Jessie felt as if she could take no more, it was over.

For a long time, they stayed motionless, each covered with a thick sheen of sweat, each afraid to break the spell they had created with their lovemaking.

# ★
# Chapter 12

"What exactly was it that you wanted to tell me last night?" Jessie asked over a plate of ham steak and eggs. "What was so all-fired important that it would cause you to ride all day, enter a lady's room in the dark of night, and have your way with her, three times."

The doctor grinned slyly over his breakfast. "Was it three?" he asked. "It seems I lost count."

"It was three," Jessie said, grinning. "I remember each one. Each and every one."

"If you say so," the young doctor replied.

"You Harvard boys are better at making love than math," Jessie said.

The doctor smiled, meeting her steady, happy gaze. But then his smile faded, but only slightly. "And may I inquire as to the state of your wound? Has it offered you any discomfort?"

Jessie blushed. "I am sore, but not from the wound," she admitted.

Her admission brought a smile to the young physician's face. But the smile vanished as suddenly as it appeared.

"Why so serious?" Jessie asked. She was still smiling. Apparently, she felt that whatever discomfort she was now experiencing was a price worth paying.

"Because I nearly forgot what I rode out to tell you," he said.

"Which is?"

"Your friend is setting that boy up," he said in a tone as serious as death. "He plans on getting him killed."

"Who, exactly, is my friend?" Jessie asked around a forkful of ham.

"Why, Sturgis, of course," Seacrest replied. Then, pulling a folded telegraph slip from his pocket, he said, "Look at this."

Jessie reached across the table, accepting the slip. Unfolding it carefully, she put it down on the table and read: "END BELLWETHER SERIES IMMEDIATELY WITH FINAL SHOWDOWN STOP READER INTEREST ON WANE STOP NEXT INSTALLMENT THE LAST STOP GG"

"See?" Seacrest asked.

"No, I don't see," Jessie replied.

"It's from his publisher in San Francisco," Seacrest said. "He wants the Bellwether Kid dead. Seems the reading public back cast is tired of him."

"I suspected as much," Jessie answered. "But you just don't kill people because nobody wants to read about them anymore."

"Oh no?" came the answer. "I went back over Sturgis's last two series of articles. Both gunfighters died. One died after only six stories. The so-called Bellwether Kid's lasted for nine installments. I'd say he has it coming, wouldn't you?"

"You can't be serious," Jessie blurted out. "He helps to kill the men he writes about?"

"Either helps or helps put them in a position where they're certain to die," Seacrest answered without any humor at all. It was by his tone that Jessie could tell he was indeed serious.

Seacrest was about to say something more when Ki came through the door. He headed straight for the table, wearing a look on his face that meant trouble was coming. "I think you should see what is going to happen," he said.

Seacrest and Jessie rose from the small table in time to see people running in the street. They all seemed to be heading toward the southern end of the town.

As they came out onto the boards, into the morning sun, Jessie could see what looked like half the town out there. They lined the street, stared through windows, and poked their heads around corners. All of them hoped to catch a glimpse of what would happen next.

Jessie knew what was going to happen. She could see it as clearly as if it were painted on canvas and hanging in a museum. The Bellwether Kid was facing off against a big man. The big man, by the looks of him, was probably a rancher.

There seemed to be some sort of dispute already in progress, though Jessie was too far away to hear. But what she saw was the big man push out, sending the Bellwether Kid staggering back with one shove of his thick hand.

Surprisingly, the Kid recovered and gathered himself up, just in time to be pushed again. This time the blow sent him sprawling in the dirt. But the fall of his opponent held no joy for the big man. He advanced, pulling his Colt revolver from its holster.

The Kid scrambled back, crablike. The big man fired, sending a shot into the dirt between the Kid's legs. When the Kid went for his gun, the big man fired a second time, sending the youth once again scrambling back.

"Are you going to try to stop it?" Seacrest asked.

Jessie shook her head sadly. It had already progressed too far. To try to stop it now was the job of a lawman. But she could see the sheriff standing off to one side, positioned on the boards. On the opposite side of the street was the girl, her mouth twisted in an agony of not fear, but anticipation.

The big man said something, and the Kid gained his feet. But even as he righted himself, the lad continued to back up, hands far away from his guns.

Then the big man said something else and holstered his Colt. When the Kid made to draw, the big man drew first, fired, and missed. A second later the Kid fired, and the big man's head exploded like a ripe melon, the bullet sending a spray of blood and brain and skull fragments out the back end. He stood for a moment, wavering in his boots, then fell heavily to the ground.

The Kid just stood there shocked and surprised, but no more shocked and surprised than the rest of the crowd. Jessie watched as the girl ran off the boards and hugged the lad. A few of the crowd let out a collective sigh, then began drifting away.

Far off down the street, leaning casually against a storefront, Jessie spotted Sturgis. He was watching the scene with almost indifference, a nasty little smile pasted across his face.

"It would appear that you were wrong," Jessie said, addressing the doctor.

"Perhaps," came the thoughtful answer. "Perhaps. But I do not think so. Something is wrong, but it isn't me."

"How many shots did you hear?" Ki asked suddenly.

"Two in the fight," Jessie said. "One from the dead man, the other from the so-called Bellwether Kid."

"I counted three shots," Ki said. "Very strange, isn't it? Very strange."

"That's just an echo," Seacrest said. "It'll happen sometimes. Shots echo off the buildings. Lot of times you can't tell for a damn who's doing the shooting."

"I do not think so," Ki replied.

Down the street, a half dozen of the sheriff's men were moving the dead man off to the side.

The sheriff himself strode off the boards, tipped his hat to the young girl, who was still hanging off the lad's neck, and began talking. Jessie couldn't hear what he was saying, but it had to be serious. She could tell that just from the way his mouth was set.

As the gawkers began to drift away, Jessie stepped off the boards and stopped one. "What happened down there?" she asked.

The man, a scrawny miner, said, "See that boy down there?"

Jessie nodded that she saw him.

"He just took on Kurt Denton," the scrawny miner said, a little wonder in his voice. "Just called him on out. Then he shot him."

"That Denton wanted for anything?"

"If he was, I don't know nothing about it," came the answer. "And there ain't much around here that I don't know about."

It didn't make sense to Jessie. She'd seen the dodger Sturgis had waved around. The dodger was for three brothers, but she couldn't remember the name. "He have any brothers?"

The miner's eyes widened some. "Just three," he said. "But they's bad ones, not like Kurt there. Kurt, he was the baby. Didn't want no part of his brothers' dealings. Those other Dentons, now, they're a bad lot."

"How bad?" Jessie asked.

The miner was quick in answering. "Well, miss, they don't come much worse. And you believe me, they are gonna be stirred up and mad as hornets when they hear about their baby brother getting shot and killed and all. That boy that done it, he ain't a friend of yours, is he?"

"Not really."

The miner's tone lightened a little. "That's good, so you won't miss him when he's killed. 'Cause them other Dentons, they gonna shoot him down like a dog."

Then the miner was gone, working his way down the street in a bowlegged walk.

"What did you hear?" Ki asked, stepping off the boards to join Jessie.

"He shot the wrong man," Jessie said. "There were four brothers. The kid shot the only one of them that wasn't a criminal."

"And the odds were with him," Ki answered. "Three out of four are good odds."

"Ki, I have the feeling it could have been ninety-nine out of one hundred, and he still would have shot the one honest man. His luck is just that bad."

Ki thought on this for a long time before making his answer. "Our luck is not much better," he said at last.

That night Sturgis found Jessie, Ki, and Seacrest enjoying a bad meal at the cafe. For her part, Jessie didn't taste any of her meal, her mind was elsewhere. She couldn't wait to get the good doctor back to her room that night.

When Sturgis approached the table, he had Peg, the sheriff's daughter, in tow. She was somber, but not sad. More than likely, she found the entire affair just too exciting for words. It was, Jessie knew, the most excitement the young girl had ever experienced.

"My good people, how fortunate that I should find you here," Sturgis said in greeting.

"Fortunate?" Jessie asked, thinking that it wasn't fortunate for her. For that matter, how lucky was it for Sturgis? There was, after all, only one cafe and two saloons in town. He could have looked into all of them in a matter of a half minute.

"Yes indeed, fortunate," Sturgis answered. "Surely, you have heard the news."

"News?" Seacrest said, just to fill space while Sturgis paused for breath.

"The news of the tragic case of mistaken identity," Sturgis said. "A horrible incident and, I might add, one freighted with all the elements of Greek drama."

"Do many people get their brains blown out the back of their heads in Greek drama, Mr. Sturgis?" Ki asked.

Sturgis seemed either not to hear or to ignore the question. "To reach the point quickly," he said, "I would appreciate, nay I would forever be in your debt, if you would offer me your eyewitness account of the gun battle."

"For publication?" Seacrest asked, chewing a portion of steak.

"Why, of course," Sturgis snapped.

"I don't believe I care to comment," Jessie said.

Ki, for his part, declined with a shake of his head.

117

"I have something for publication," Seacrest said.

Sturgis leaned in close, waiting anxiously to catch every word. "But your comments are welcome, invited even," he said in a soothing voice. "Why, the words of a humble country doctor, intimate and confidant to those whose pain he has relieved and whose babies he has birthed. What better witness? Who could be more possessed of simple country wisdom or on more intimate terms with life and death in this harsh yet promising country?"

Seacrest finished chewing his food and swallowed before answering. "I won't make a speech," he said. "Just deliver a message."

"A message?" Sturgis asked, puzzled.

Seacrest dug into his pocket and pulled out the telegram and handed it to Sturgis.

The reporter read it slowly. It wasn't until he was finished that all the blood drained from his face and his fist crumpled the paper into a ball. Still holding the ball, he stormed out of the cafe without saying a word.

★

# Chapter 13

Jessie, Ki, and Seacrest arrived at a general plan sometime after breakfast. The plan included Jessie's purchase of two horses, a good supper, and a night of lovemaking with the doctor. Carson City now was only two days' ride, and with any luck at all, they'd be able to make it there and back and be on their way to Texas within three days.

It took the better part of the afternoon to find two suitable horses. The livery owner made much of the fact that Jessie didn't know the country, the people, and their horse-trading ways. She was, he assured her, about to make a costly mistake by not purchasing the horses directly from him. But Jessie figured that people were people and horse-trading was horse-trading wherever you went. And besides, buying the horses would fill what remained of the day.

They found the horses in early afternoon. A pair of sorrels that rode well and appeared to be sweet-mouthed. Jessie figured that they'd not only complete the two-day journey, but she'd be able to earn a profit from them in Carson City, where horse prices were higher.

They managed to make it back to town ahead of dark and return the buggy to the livery man, who admitted they'd got a good price for the pair of matched sorrels.

"Well, that was a fair piece of work for one day," Jessie said as she, Ki, and Seacrest crossed back to the cafe.

"Not bad," Seacrest offered.

Ki, for his part, remained silent. He was still puzzling over the mysterious second shot he had heard during the shoot-out.

It was after dinner, and Jessie had retired to her room. She left the door unlocked, expecting Seacrest, who had figured that maybe a beer or two was what was required before retiring for the evening.

Jessie stripped off her clothes and reclined on the bed, turning the lamp down low. The doctor, she knew, would be a matter of minutes, and she wanted to be ready. After all, it was their last night together. Tomorrow they'd be heading off in opposite directions. And there was something more than a little sad about that. Last nights together were inevitably sad, and the fact that the doctor was one the best lovers she'd ever had only made it sadder still.

Jessie was lying on top of the covers, toying with the idea that perhaps she'd forgo the train for one last chance with the doctor on her way home, when the door opened.

The creak of the old hinges pulled Jessie out of her dreams. At last, the good doctor had arrived and in less time than she'd expected.

Jessie rolled over, arranging herself on the bed to give the doctor more room. She could feel the air from the open door on her face, feel his presence enter the room. "You're early," she whispered. "I didn't expect you so soon."

When she didn't hear footsteps, she turned. The figure at the door stood stock-still, then made a sudden movement with his right hand, bringing it up from his side.

A sharp jolt of panic hit Jessie, and she rolled, throwing herself to the floor as five shots rang out, the bullets plowing into the pillow and scattering feathers.

Jessie's hand flew toward the pillow, under which was the .38 with the peach-wood grips. The gunman fired again, but the gun clicked on empty as Jessie brought the revolver up and fired.

Her shot went wild, piercing the door frame as the gunman fled from the open door. Jessie, a blanket wrapped around her, leapt to her feet and gave chase. But even as she reached the door, the running steps were already retreating down the narrow hall, toward the back door.

A second later men were rushing toward her, drinkers, other guests at the hotel, a few loiterers from out front. They stood there mute before her. They had rushed to the shots fully expecting to see a dead man, not a live, half-dressed woman holding a gun.

"What are you all looking at?" Jessie asked defiantly, raising the gun for emphasis.

"It would just be a guess, but I'd say you," came a familiar voice at her back.

Jessie turned to face Seacrest, who was standing not three feet behind her with an amused smile on his face. He'd come up the opposite stairway, no doubt.

"And you wouldn't be lyin', either," one of the gawkers offered. "Not lyin' a bit."

It only took a few minutes for Seacrest to break up the knot of gawkers and usher Jessie back to her room. Once inside, he examined the bed under close lamplight, then carefully dug one of the bullets from the frame with a penknife.

"Looks to me like a .44," he said.

"Well, that about narrows it down to only half the men in town," she answered, collapsing dejectedly across the bullet-riddled mattress and ruined pillow.

"But you didn't get a good look at him, did you?" Seacrest asked, taking a seat himself.

"As I said before, I thought it was you," Jessie answered. "Same height and build."

"And all cats are gray in the dark, is that it?"

"All gunmen are, anyway," she shot back.

Taking the gun from her hand, he said, "Let's us just discuss this in the morning, shall we?"

Jessie felt the gun slide from her fingers. "Sheriff will more than likely be here any second now."

"Not a chance," Seacrest corrected. "In these towns it ain't against the law to shoot up a mattress. Not one bit."

"Someone tried to kill me," Jessie said. "Maybe we should go see him."

Seacrest put his arm around her, drawing Jessie close as he pulled her back on the bed. When he finally spoke, his face was very close to her own. "Now, you don't intend to pull the only law in town out of a perfectly fine bed to look at a shot-up bed, do you?"

"Attempted murder isn't against the law, I suppose?"

Seacrest edged the blanket down with one finger, exposing her breasts. "The gunman's gone," he whispered, bringing his mouth closer. "The bed will still be shot tomorrow, and the murder will be just as attempted."

"I suppose," Jessie answered, closing her eyes as the doctor fastened his lips around her nipple.

"Mmmm," Seacrest said, playfully poking and caressing her hardening nipple with his tongue.

Jessie opened her mouth slightly and heard herself purr softly.

"You are a beautiful woman," the doctor said, releasing the hard nipple to the cool air as he took the other one between his lips.

As he toyed and teased her nipple, Jessie reached down and began to work at his belt. To her surprise, he was wearing a gunbelt. Why hadn't she noticed that earlier? She undid it and pulled it off him from behind, raising it just high enough to peek over his shoulder and see that it was a Colt .44. A chill of panic ran through her, then she let it slide from her grasp to the floor.

Seacrest released her nipple and eased down,

letting his tongue trail downward, tracing a delightfully moist path down her silky flesh.

When his journey had progressed just below her breasts, she reached down and toyed with the hair at the back of his head, grown just over the collar of his collarless shirt.

"Oh, that feels so, so nice," she purred as his tongue made its way across her below. "So, very, very nice."

A moment later, his tongue was tracing a path across the top of her silky hair. Every nerve in her body seemed to hum and vibrate, like telegraph wires in a slight breeze. Every cell in her body hungered for his touch.

Soon he was moving across the soft tuft of hair, his lips pulling gently at the curly mass as his mouth worked its way deliberately around the edges. She felt the tickle of his cheeks against the insides of her thighs, the touch of his hands resting gently at her hips. She drank it in, drank in every teasing touch like some giant glass of sweet punch.

Then he was working his way inward, his mouth—those full lips—working their way to the moist and waiting crevice. Jessie opened her legs wide, dangling one foot off the edge of the bed.

Kneeling between her long coltish legs, he poked his tongue out, and she felt a shiver of delightful pleasure run through her. He did it again, this time higher up, and another delightful shiver ran through her. Oh, he was good, she thought. Perhaps even the best lover she'd ever taken. Certainly better than anything she had expected or hoped to find in Nevada.

His tongue was teasing her again, moving now from the center of her tuft to the sides. Using just the very tip, he let it wander far down, then up across one side, just at the edge of her silky patch, before his lips took hold of and pulled at the soaking hair.

"Now," she said, almost pleading. "Please, now, now, now. Please do it now."

The doctor was only too happy to oblige. Rising up, he unfastened his trousers as Jessie arranged herself on all fours. Coming up behind her, he ran the tip of his swollen member up the inside of her smooth thigh, then gently rubbed it against the waiting crevice.

She shifted slightly, moving back against Seacrest, then reached behind and guided him into her. Jessie felt his hands go to her hips, but she did not move. For a long while they stayed frozen like that, joined together and perfectly still.

"Is this the way you want it?" he asked. "Me with my boots on?"

"Yes," she said. "I want you any way. But mostly I want you fast. And I want you now!"

He began moving for an answer, sinking himself completely into her, then pausing before pulling back. When all but the very end of him was withdrawn, he moved forward again, slowly.

Jessie felt her hips begin to move, following his slow, steady strokes. Soon she felt her breasts swaying, first forward and back, then little by little side to side. Still damp from his clever tongue, they tingled in the cool air as they moved.

As his movements increased in speed, he removed his hand from her hip and brought it around the front. Capturing one of her full breasts in the palm of his hand, he began to teasingly pull and turn it with two fingers.

She felt him on top of her. The material of his shirt against her bare back, the rub of of his pants with each thrust into her.

In a short time it wasn't just Jessie and the good doctor who were rocking back and forth; the bed was moving as well. With each thrust and wriggle, the old wood-framed bed creaked and swayed. Its legs rubbed and jumped along the rough floor.

And then Jessie felt herself reaching the peak. She matched each of Seacrest's thrusts, pushing back against him as he buried himself in her. Lowering her head to the mass of feathers, she wriggled and rolled back against him, urging his release as well as her own.

As the first hard, warm waves of pleasure washed over her, Jessie felt the doctor's grip tighten as he began his release. Reaching his hand around, his fingers sought out the most sensitive place in her soft tuft, so that she had to bite down on the half-filled pillow to keep from screaming her pleasure.

Then she felt his release, and she pushed harder against his thrusts. When they were both at their height, the bed's joints gave a pitiful creak as the boards came unpegged at the front, collapsing the bed and sending him yet deeper into her.

They collapsed across the tilted and ruined bed, feathers clinging to their sweat-soaked skin. And that's where they fell asleep, Jessie and Seacrest, before he'd even slipped out of her.

★

# Chapter 14

Jessie and Seacrest were awakened by a knock on the door. They opened their eyes together, the knocking ceased, and the door opened. And there, standing in the doorway, was the sheriff, Ki positioned directly behind him.

"Good lordy, what you folks been doing in here, anyways?" the sheriff asked. He was a fat man, but not particularly jolly. His badge was pinned to a sweat-stained vest that stretched out over his expanse of belly.

"Do you make it a habit to enter a lady's room uninvited?" Jessie asked, pulling the blanket up around her feather-covered breasts.

"Figured in your case I'd make an exception," the lawman said, still surveying the damage. "Seeing as I heard about the shooting last night."

"Jessie, are you hurt?" Ki asked, already knowing the answer. Perhaps her pride was hurt, but nothing else.

The sheriff took another step into the room, hooked his thumbs into the belt of his stretched trousers, and said, "They done a good job on the bed. Shot up the pillows, mattress, busted the leg. How they bust that leg, missy?"

Jessie didn't answer, but rather stared at the lawman with total contempt. She'd seen his kind before. He was that breed of law who figured as long as it was strangers getting shot in his town, then it didn't matter so much. Not like a citizen getting shot at, which would have been a different story.

"That bed's got a busted leg," he said, drawing out his ancient Navy Colt. "You figure I should shoot it?"

"Sheriff, I would suggest, very strongly, that you leave," Seacrest said, pausing only briefly to wipe a feather from his mouth.

"We will meet you in the cafe," Ki suggested, then began edging the sheriff back out the door.

"Damn, but if you don't look good in feathers, missy," the lawman said as he was hustled out the door. "Like an angel or something. But I don't figure you was acting like no angel. Was you?"

"How I act is none of your concern," Jessie snapped.

"Angels don't go round busting up beds in dollar-a-night hotels, now do they?"

When the sheriff and Ki were safely out the door, Jessie turned to Seacrest, raised her hands above her head, and screamed, "How I hate this place!"

Seacrest watched intently as the blanket fell,

revealing two perfectly shaped breasts nearly completely covered in feathers. He stared for a split second, but only managed to hold a look of serious empathy on his face for another moment before he burst out laughing.

"It's not funny!" Jessie snapped.

"Oh, it's pretty funny," Seacrest countered.

And Jessie had to agree. A second later she, too, burst into laughter.

It took Jessie nearly a full half hour to pluck every last feather from her person. Some of them, she was startled to find, had lodged in the most embarrassing places. If it had not been for the good doctor's help, she might have walked around all day with feathers stuck to her.

They found Ki down the street, at the cafe. The sheriff had long departed, not caring much to wait more than ten minutes if someone, particularly a voter, hadn't actually been murdered.

"Have you discovered anything, Ki?" Jessie asked, taking a seat opposite him.

"Just that the Dentons will be arriving soon," he said. "Two men rode out to tell them this morning. They should be in town by tonight to claim the body."

"That doesn't concern us," Jessie answered. "I figure we could be out of town in an hour."

Seacrest eyed her skeptically. "Not wondering about who shot up your bed, then?"

"Not much," Jessie said. "Could have been anything. I don't even know if they were looking for me or someone else."

"Sounds a little like you're running," Seacrest offered.

"Leaving a fight that isn't your own isn't running," Jessie said.

Ki raised an eyebrow at this, but said nothing. The way that he viewed the situation, maybe Jessie's now-healed wound hadn't counted for anything, but the moment her bed was shot, the fight had become her own.

"And don't you give me that look, either, Ki," she added hastily. "You want to leave as much as anyone. Just let's get ourselves out of here and be done with it."

For an answer, she received only a resigned shrug.

A few minutes later they were leaving the cafe, walking out onto the boards. The street was nearly empty, a few horses and buckboards passing. Across the way, in front of the saloon and livery, loiterers had set themselves up to pass the day.

Ki was still silent, not caring to comment on Jessie's decision, but accepting it all the same. If she wanted to leave, then that was her choice, and he would follow as he always had.

It was as they were crossing the street that the shot rang out. Jessie heard it clearly, a far-off shot that sent her falling to the ground and brought her gun out in a flash. Out of the corner of her eye she saw Ki and Seacrest take similar actions.

When no other shots came, she silently chided herself for panicking, but didn't put the gun away. "You okay, Ki?" she said, pulling herself to her feet.

"Yes, I am not hurt," came the answer.

"Doc, how about you?" she asked, turning back to the doctor.

Seacrest was still lying on the ground, a hand wrapped around his holstered pistol.

"Doc!" Jessie yelled, getting to her feet quickly.

She ran the two steps to Seacrest, who lay motionless on the ground. "Doc!" she cried again, and when he didn't move, she turned him over. A bright red stain of blood had blossomed just left from the center of his chest.

A moment later Ki was at her side. He examined Seacrest quickly. "He's dead, Jessie," Ki said. "Someone shot him through the heart."

"Damn it, Ki," Jessie spat, getting to her feet and running her eyes across the opposite side of the street. "Damn it, now it is personal."

From all around men were approaching hesitantly, pulled to the body by curiosity. Soon Jessie found herself standing in the middle of the street, next to the dead doctor, surrounded by the curious.

Off at the edge of the crowd, she caught a glimpse of a familiar brown suit. Pushing her way through the gawking men, she made a beeline for Sturgis, who began backing up in retreat the moment he saw her approach.

"Hold it, Sturgis," she yelled, but the reporter had already turned and was walking swiftly away.

The crowd parted for Jessie, and she brought her unholstered gun up. "Hold it, Mr. Sturgis!" she ordered. When he failed to stop, she fired, the bullet sending up a puff of dirt not three inches from his left foot.

Sturgis froze. For a full second he didn't turn, but when he finally did, he was almost smiling. "Miss Starbuck," he said, greeting her soberly with a touch to his hat.

"And just what do you know about this?" Jessie demanded.

The reporter looked past Jessie, toward the crowd and the body of the dead doctor. His gaze was a professional one, well accustomed to viewing fatal follies and bloody foibles. "Horrible business, just horrible," he said. "You have my deepest sympathy."

Jessie's eyes shot to the reporter's waist, where she noticed he wasn't wearing a gun. "Where is he?" she demanded.

"He?" Sturgis asked, almost genuinely confused.

"The Bellwether Kid or whatever you're calling him today," she spat back. "Where the hell is he?"

"Why, Miss Starbuck, surely you don't believe—you can't be serious in imagining he had anything to do with this."

"Sturgis, save all those words for someone who'll pay you for them," Jessie said angrily. "Just tell me where he is!"

The reporter hesitated for a moment, then said, "I believe he's taken lodging at the establishment known as Miss Zim's."

"He's at the whorehouse," someone behind Jessie called.

"Where is it?" Jessie asked, turning to the crowd, which had abandoned the body to watch the confrontation with Sturgis.

"End of the street," one of the gawkers offered.

"Last building," another said.

Jessie turned and headed off down the street, Ki running to catch up with her. "Jessie, it would appear you have an audience," he said when he was at her side.

Turning, she saw that, indeed, she did have an audience. Ten or twelve of the men had fallen in step behind her, like a parade. A couple had remained behind to look at poor Seacrest.

When they finally reached the whorehouse, a one-story building with a narrow porch, Jessie, her gun still drawn, stomped up the two front steps and through the door.

The gawkers waited in the street, out of respect for Miss Zim and fearful that to follow the crazy lady from Texas into the whorehouse in the middle of the morning would result in their banishment.

# ★
# Chapter 15

Inside the whorehouse's door was a modest parlor. Three or four whores lounged, half-awake, on chairs and a pair of velvet settees so battered and worn that they looked as if they'd been dragged behind a mule team from New Orleans.

"Where is that son of a bitch?" Jessie said by way of announcing herself.

One of the whores, a fat woman in gray drawers, answered back, "Which son of a bitch would that be? We got nothing but bastards, whores, and sonsabitches here. Enough of each and too many of some."

Ki, stepping in front of Jessie, asked, "The gentleman who calls himself the Bellwether Kid."

"Oh, that one," the whore answered. "He's out back, shacked up in a crib with a girl. Hotel won't take 'em, so they rented out a crib."

Jessie didn't reply; rather she strode by the big woman and through the kitchen to the back porch. Beyond the porch were a group of scraggly chickens scratching in the dirt for the last of the morning's feed, and beyond them a collection of shacks. The shacks looked for all the world like elongated outhouses. Indeed, an outhouse stood in the center of them, conveniently located so that the whores could empty their slop buckets without traveling too far.

Jessie took the two steps off the porch in a single stride, scattering the chickens as she headed toward the first crib. From behind her she heard the fat lady yell, "Last one, over there on the left! Don't want you busting in on one a my girls. Lord knows they need their rest."

Changing course, Jessie doubled back, scattering the chickens again, and drew her gun. She approached the crib and knocked once, then raised a booted foot and kicked the door in. The ill-fitting door gave way under the impact and went swinging back to the wall. Inside was darkness.

"Come out here, you bastard!" Jessie called into the dark room, but as her eyes grew accustomed to the dim light, she could see that the room was empty.

"He isn't here, Ki," Jessie shouted back to Ki, who shrugged. Then, turning back to the fat lady, she said, "Where'd he go?"

"You asking me?" she replied. "You asking me like I'd know or care?"

Jessie, gun still drawn, took a step into the room. The small shack was empty except for a bed and a slop bucket. No bag, no tack, nothing

136

to indicate it had been used for anything except housing whores. "You sure this is the one you rented him?"

"I tell you it's the one, then it's the one," came the answer. "This ain't no San Francisco hotel, it's a whorehouse and a damn good one. People come and go. Ain't my business to keep track, 'cept for the money. And don't be waking up my girls, neither. If he ain't in that there one, he ain't here."

Jessie holstered her Colt and returned to the porch and Ki. "Well, damn, must have just missed him," she said. "Must have left right after shooting the doc."

"Maybe," Ki answered, not wanting to commit to Jessie's theory. "Perhaps we should search for him at the livery."

Jessie silently took Ki's advice and headed back up the back porch and out through the parlor, the way she had come. By the time she reached the street, a small group of men were waiting for her. And a few of the whores had followed her out, wanting to see what all the commotion was about.

"It would appear we have attracted attention," Ki said as Jessie stormed down the street, her head held high.

Ki's statement was another one of his masterful understatements. Following behind them were at least a half dozen men and a few curious whores.

The livery owner met them at the door. Grimly, he announced that the Bellwether Kid had packed up and rode out not an hour before. "Took that pretty little girl with him, too," the livery man said.

No sooner had he spoken than there was a disturbance at the back of the crowd. Jessie turned to see Sturgis pushing his way through.

"Is it true?" the reporter asked. "Is what these good people told me true? That our young friend has departed once again?"

Jessie, in a rage, drew her gun and pulled Sturgis to her by the front of his shirt. Pressing the Colt's barrel against the tip of his chin, she said, "It's true. And I'll tell you something else that's true."

"And what would that be, my dear Miss Starbuck?" Sturgis asked with some difficulty.

"Since you seem to be such an expert on him, you're gonna take us to your Bellwether Kid."

Sturgis's eyes looked around him in a panic, though they found not one sympathetic face. A slow, grim nod from Ki confirmed beyond all doubt Jessie's plan.

"Miss Starbuck, I would be pleased to offer my assistance in the locating of our young friend," Sturgis offered. "We shall leave as soon—"

"We'll ride out today, right now," Jessie demanded, still not releasing him.

"Exactly, precisely what I was just about to offer," Sturgis replied. "An excellent plan. And if I might say, totally in agreement with my own. We'll ride out as soon as—"

"Soon as you can climb on a damned horse," Jessie said, releasing him roughly.

• • •

They were out of town within the hour, Jessie in such a rush that Ki barely had time to purchase supplies from the general merchandise. Sturgis, for his part, remained oddly silent until the town had passed behind them. It was only after the last confusion of tracks from wheel and horse were gone from the trail that Sturgis ventured to speak.

"Miss Starbuck, if I may inquire as to your destination?" he asked timidly.

"My destination, Mr. Sturgis, is the Bellwether Kid," Jessie shot back.

"And in what direction do you feel your greatest chances for success point?"

"Let's just see about that when we get there," Jessie said. In truth, she had only a vague plan. She didn't know anything about the gunfighter, except he was the strangest gunman she'd ever seen. But she knew women, and she knew for certain that the girl Peg wouldn't be happy pointed toward some small town. No, a girl like that, away from home for the first time and looking for excitement, would want to head toward Carson City, the biggest town within two days' ride.

To his dubious credit, Sturgis did not begin to complain until almost nightfall. But when he started in to bellyaching, he did it with a vengeance. The trail was too rough, the horse turning lame, the weather damp, the saddle malformed, and most of all, his stomach empty.

Jessie relented to the reporter's request to make camp as the last light vanished over the hills. Not wanting to risk a night ride over an unfamiliar trail, she pulled off into the brush and found a camp a hundred yards from a small rock stream.

They were ground-staking their horses when Ki suddenly tensed, his head coming up like a deer's upwind from a hunter.

"Ki, what is it?" Jessie asked.

"I thought I heard something," came his answer in a whisper.

Jessie listened intently, but could hear nothing.

"It sounded like someone moving about in the brush," Ki said, still listening. "Someone close."

Jessie made herself perfectly still, but could not hear a thing. Her eyes searched the already darkening landscape, but to no avail.

"Really, don't you think this is carrying this entire business too far?" Sturgis said suddenly. "Who would possibly follow us? Who would want to?"

Jessie slipped her Colt from its holster and aimed it at the reporter. "One more word," she whispered. "One more word and you'll never find out."

"I will look," Ki said, then pulled a *shuriken* from the small sack on his belt and slipped silently off into the darkness.

Both Jessie and Sturgis watched as Ki melted into the night. For a long time neither said a word, then Jessie slipped her gun back into its holster and said, "Why don't you go get us some wood for a fire?"

"You can't seriously expect me to trample about out there," came the weak reply.

"Mr. Sturgis," Jessie answered, making the name sound like an insult. "From now on I expect you to do whatever I tell you. And to do it quickly. Now, go back down toward the trail and bring back some of that deadfall I saw on the way up here."

Sturgis left, crashing through the brush and mumbling the entire time.

Jessie was just glad to be rid of him. The man had become an annoyance, even when he wasn't talking. He was so much of an annoyance in fact that she was seriously wondering why she had brought him along.

Ki returned before Sturgis, coming cautiously into camp from the trees. Just by the look on his face Jessie could tell he was worried.

"Well, did you see anything?" she asked, getting the kindling together for the fire.

"Someone was out there," he answered. "Very close. He was watching us. I found tracks, broken branches fifteen yards away from where you are now standing."

"Did you see him? See anyone?" Jessie asked, rising from her work on the fire.

"No, but I heard him," Ki said. "Whoever it is, he knows the forest. He knows how to move through it."

"Could be a miner, someone with a claim nearby."

"It could be, but I do not think so," Ki answered. "I believe he was following us. Where is Sturgis?"

"I sent him off to get wood," Jessie said. "He went off toward the trail. It wasn't him you heard, was it?"

"Opposite direction. I followed him upstream, then lost him. Then he just vanished."

Sturgis returned then, burdened under a heavy armload of deadfall branches. He practically fell out of the darkness of the tree line and into the camp. "Here's your damned firewood," he wheezed. "Take it and be done with it. And I sincerely hope that you take pride in sending a man of my skills, a celebrated scribe, into the wilderness like a witless servant so that you may have your morning coffee."

The outburst was so out of character that it took Jessie back a second. "Little out of sorts, are we?" she asked, taunting.

"Miss Starbuck, physical labor is not one of my strong suits," came the reply. "Had you devoted any time to the matter at all, you could not but have guessed that it would do nothing to improve my mood."

Jessie couldn't help but smile. Finally, she had found something that annoyed Sturgis as much as the reporter annoyed her.

★

# Chapter 16

Jessie awoke to the smell of fresh coffee. Opening her eyes, she saw Ki squatting across the fire and feeding a large branch into the flames, his eyes moving steadily into the trees. Sturgis was nowhere in sight.

"Where's our friend?" she asked, stretching out of her bedroll and pulling a boot on.

"Gone," Ki replied, pushing the entire length of wood into the fire.

"Gone where?" Jessie asked, figuring that the reporter had awakened a few minutes earlier and wandered into the trees to relieve himself.

"He ran off in the middle of the night," Ki answered. "Quiet as a mouse. But left a trail a blind man could follow. And he left without his horse. His bags and bedroll are still here."

It took a second for the news to sink in. The reporter's hasty departure was more than just a way to avoid work. Jessie, now fully awake and dressed, joined Ki at the fire. Pouring a cup of coffee, she said, "It's strange, isn't it?"

"Yes, it is," Ki replied. "It is very strange. But then, this entire matter has been very strange. I do not believe I have ever seen anything like it, even a little."

Jessie thought on it a long while, sipping at the hot coffee and listening to the morning birds. "He's meeting someone," she said at last. "He has to be. Maybe whoever was out there last night. But a man doesn't walk off without his gear in the middle of nowhere. Not even someone as useless as Sturgis."

"Perhaps it is possible he just walked back to town."

"He's too lazy for it," Jessie said, taking another sip of coffee. But this one was incautious; caught in thought, she'd forgotten how hot it was. Startled by burning her tongue, she fumbled the cup, causing her to flinch and spill coffee over her hand. As she jerked her hand, a far-off shot rang out and the cup was torn from her fingers.

Ki reacted instantly. Moving in a blur, he knocked Jessie sideways, bringing her to the ground just as another shot exploded from the trees. A thick column of sparks shot upward at the center of the fire as the bullet furrowed into the flame and ash.

"The trees!" Jessie yelled, and began running in a crouch, Ki right behind her. Two more shots followed them, sending dirt flying up at their boot heels.

When they were safely behind the cover of two thick pines, Ki turned to Jessie and dug a *shuriken* out of the small pouch on his waist. Using hand signals, he indicated that he was going to head back behind them and circle around. The gunman was in front of them, nearly dead center, judging from the shots.

Jessie, her gun out, peeked around the side of one of the trees and nodded. A portion of bark splintered at her cheek, sending her back behind the thick tree for cover.

As Ki crept back, Jessie fired three fast shots in the general direction of the gunman. With any luck at all, she'd send him behind the nearest cover, so he wouldn't notice Ki's departure.

The horses were ground-staked ten yards away, out in the open. To try for one of them would be suicide. The packs were in a worse position, far out in the center of the small camp. Jessie would be dead before she took three steps into the open.

"Who are you?" she called.

A moment later the gunman gave his answer, burying a bullet dead center in the tree. Well, at least she could be fairly certain it wasn't Sturgis. Sturgis being able to shoot would not have surprised her all that much. But his keeping quiet long enough to shoot would have surprised the hell out of her.

Ki had been gone maybe fifteen minutes before Jessie chose to peek out around the tree again. When she did, no shot came from the trees in front of her. The coffee in the pot on the fire had burned down; now an acrid smoke began drifting from the top.

"You still out there?" she called.

But no answer came back.

Firing twice more, she crept out around the tree. Somehow, deep in her bones, she felt it safe. With the Colt still out, she walked cautiously up to the fire and pulled the coffeepot off with a branch.

Somewhere, out in the dense trees, Ki was there. She knew he could stalk noiselessly, even through the driest brush. She didn't fear for him; at least Ki had the cover of trees and his warrior ways. But she just felt out in the open, even though she knew that to venture into the brush meant scaring the gunman or gunmen. No, it was better to let Ki stalk the prey in his own manner.

Suddenly Jessie felt a chill run up her back. It might have been a breeze too gentle to feel, but whatever it was, it made the fine blond hairs on the back of her neck stand up. Spinning, she brought the Colt up, ready to fire. But as her eyes searched the green, she saw nothing.

Walking back to the tree, she heard a slight crack, like a branch breaking. The sound froze Jessie in her tracks.

Backing up against the tree, she broke open the Colt's cylinder and released all five spent cartridges into her palm. She was pulling fresh cartridges from her belt, cursing herself for not braving the walk to the horses, when she heard another sound. Then, from behind the tree, not ten feet in front of her, he stepped.

The sight of him froze her as much as the fact that he'd startled her. The stranger was tall, well over six feet, and dressed in what looked like a country preacher's castoffs. But what held her attention, even more than the fancy rifle, with all the scrollwork, he held in one hand, and even more than the Navy Colt he pointed at her from the other, was that he was half-red. And not red like an Indian, either. But fully one half of his lean, sunken face, and perhaps one half of his entire skinny body, was bright red, like a birthmark.

"Howdy, Miss Starbuck," he said, the words coming out in a thick Southern drawl from a nearly toothless mouth.

"Who are you?" Jessie asked. "What do you want?"

"Don't matter, Miss Starbuck," he answered. "Really, it ain't even none of your affair, except the part about me killing you."

Jessie was about to say something else. Talk was the only option now, what with him holding the Colt on her and her own gun empty.

The stranger was raising the Colt for a shot when Jessie caught a flash of light.

An instant later the tall man twitched, his head flying to one side, a *shuriken*'s point buried deep in his temple. The rifle dropped from his hand as he tried to claw the throwing star from his head, but the Colt kept coming up, rising uneasily as his eyes widened with surprise at the numbing pain.

There was another flash of light, and another *shuriken* buried itself in him, this one in his neck. A thick spurt of blood erupted. But the gun kept coming up.

147

Jessie snapped the cylinder of her gun closed and fired. The hammer clicked on an empty chamber as the gunman shook, quivering. A spasm in his finger brought the trigger back, sending an explosion of dirt between Jessie's feet. She pulled back on the trigger again, stepping sideways, and the gun fired, sending a round solidly into the gunman's throat and exploding out the back.

For what seemed like a long time the gunman stood uneasily, then he toppled to the left, falling in a heap.

A second later Ki emerged from the trees, another *shuriken* in his hand and a puzzled look on his face.

"Now, who in hell is that?" Jessie asked, taking a step closer.

"I do not know," Ki replied, replacing the *shuriken* in his pouch.

Jessie could see now that the gunman was almost impossibly thin. Over six feet tall and he could not have weighed more than a hundred and thirty pounds. The loss of blood gave his face a weird cast, making the birthmark stand out sharply against the white, bloodless skin.

Kneeling down, she took the Colt from the dead man's hand and tossed it away. It was the rifle that held her attention. Lifting it off the ground where he'd dropped it, she gave it a careful inspection as Ki moved toward her to get a better look.

The gun was a Remington Long Range Creedmoor, of the .44-caliber variety. It had a single-set trigger, a Vernier sight mounted on the tang, and a globe front sight. The stock was carved walnut, but all the trimmings were done up in silver. The gun weighed heavily in her hands. She knew it was perhaps the finest long-range rifle in the world.

"Well, what do you think, Ki?" she asked, handing him the rifle.

"I think that this is probably the man who fired the second shot I heard," came the answer.

"When would that be? When Seacrest was shot?"

"Seacrest, Denton, everyone we've seen the Bellwether Kid kill."

"It would certainly make sense," Jessie confirmed. "Damned good sense, if you ask me."

"And we both know just the person capable of such a deceit," Ki replied.

Before Jessie could answer with the obvious name, Sturgis came running from the trees in panic. "Oh, thank all the good graces that you haven't been killed!" he yelled as he came running toward them, out of breath.

Jessie turned to the voice, her empty gun still out, though she was confident she wouldn't need a gun to take care of the reporter. "This your friend?" she asked.

"Heavens no!" Sturgis exclaimed. He looked more than a little repulsed by the carnage. "Who is he?"

"We were about to ask you," Ki said flatly.

"I went off in total darkness to relieve myself this morning and became lost," Sturgis blurted out by way of excuse. "Horrible business. I shouted myself hoarse. Then someone, him I suppose or his comrades in villainy, knocked me out cold. Came up behind and hit me on the head. When I woke up, my disorientation had grown, as you can well imagine. I wouldn't have found you at all—"

"Convenient that you should find your way back just after the shooting," Jessie said, her voice thick with sarcasm and suspicion.

"The point exactly!" Sturgis said with no little enthusiasm. "I followed the noise and—"

"Here you are," Ki finished, his tone completely and utterly skeptical.

"Exactly, my dear friends," Sturgis concluded. "Now, if you don't mind my asking, who is this miserable wretch?"

★

# Chapter 17

They rode out as soon as they could break camp and bury the body. Jessie and Ki, by unspoken agreement, decided to play along with Sturgis's pathetic story. For the immediate future, it was easier than beating the truth out of the reporter. Though, as they rode, both kept their hands close to weapons. There was no way of telling if Sturgis had more gunmen out in the hills.

"If I may be so bold as to—"

"Please, Mr. Sturgis, don't be," Jessie snapped at him.

"And to what do I owe your shabby mood, Miss Starbuck?" Sturgis persisted.

Jessie took her time in answering, not bothering to turn toward Sturgis. "Well, Mr. Sturgis," she began. "I suppose you could chalk it up to someone shooting at me. Or maybe it's the fact that I'm missing two horses I paid for twice. It could also be that an intimate friend of mine was gunned down for no reason. And maybe, just maybe, Mr. Sturgis, it's the fact that digging shallow graves in rocky soil before breakfast just usually puts me in a bad mood."

"None of which, I would remind you, was the direct consequence of my actions."

"And while we're at it, Mr. Byron Sturgis, suppose you explain that telegraph message," Jessie said. "The one that mentioned you ending the Bellwether Kid's exploits."

"Nothing to explain, really," came the smooth answer. "Simply a business decision by my colleagues back east. Apparently my loyal readership has grown somewhat bored with his exploits."

"So that's what those Dentons were about, wasn't it?" Jessie chided. "What were you planning—to kill him yourself or have one of those brothers take care of it?"

"Nothing of the kind," Sturgis said, and then he began to pout.

Two or three miles down the trail, Jessie decided she liked the pouting Sturgis better. For one thing, he was quiet.

They were just rounding a bend in the trail, one side a sheer rock wall, the other a sloping drop of a hundred feet, when they heard the shot.

Jessie reined in her horse and looked past Sturgis to Ki. "Less than a mile," Ki said. "Perhaps much less."

Pulling the Colt from its holster, Jessie spurred the horse gently. It wouldn't due to ride into trouble too quickly, but it seemed as if there were no avoiding it now.

A quarter mile or so beyond the bend, they saw the trouble. The Bellwether Kid and the sheriff's daughter, Peg, were tying the remains of a horse with a length of rope. A large black-and-red hole bloomed at the center of the animal's head. The young man barely looked up from his work.

"Afternoon, Miss Starbuck, Mr. Sturgis," the young gunman said. He could have been greeting them on the street for all the concern his voice showed.

"Mind telling me what happened to my horse?" Jessie asked, her voice forced down to calm through some extraordinary act of will.

"Threw a shoe, split its hoof, broke its leg," the young man answered matter-of-factly as he led the other horse forward off the trail. "Hope you didn't spend too much on it. Every dime more than fifty dollars you got charged was like stealing. Just exactly like it."

Jessie watched as the young man pulled the animal off the trail and knelt to untie the ropes. "Ever think that what you did *was* stealing?"

"That's strictly speaking," he answered back. "I was gonna leave both animals in Carson City for you."

"And that's all you have to say for yourself?" Jessie hissed through clenched teeth. "That's all you have to say after stealing my horses, not to mention the sheriff's daughter?"

"I'm marrying age," the girl said, somewhat too

proudly. "Marrying age and then some."

"Got something else to say, then I said all I plan to," the boy offered. "Mr. Sturgis, I quit. I ain't gonna be the Bellwether Kid no more."

"What are you talking about, boy?" Sturgis answered, rising up in the saddle. "Why, you're a legend now. A living legend."

"No future in being a legend," the lad replied. "I'm going back to being Horace Gatz."

"You were working for Sturgis?" Jessie asked incredulously as she climbed down off her horse. She wanted to talk to Gatz or the Bellwether Kid or whatever he called himself, eyeball to eyeball.

"Only in a manner of speaking," Sturgis said.

"If taking money from him and doing what he says all the time is working for him, then I was," Horace Gatz answered.

"He treated Horace badly, Miss Starbuck," the girl put in.

"Made me wear these clothes for one," Gatz said.

"Just answer me one thing," Jessie asked. "Did you shoot those men or did Sturgis arrange that, too?"

"Miss Starbuck, I hardly never shot at nobody, much less hit anybody," Gatz said. "Abel did all the shooting. One time I did try to shoot, I hit you. And I'm sick sorry about that, too."

Sensing that the game was up, Sturgis suddenly spurred his horse, turning it awkwardly on the trail. By the time Jessie was back on her own animal, he'd vanished around the bend.

Sturgis was a better rider than she would have guessed. He didn't have much of a lead on her, but he had enough. Somewhere behind her, she heard Ki galloping up.

When she finally caught up with Sturgis, it was with his horse's hoofbeats vanishing into the distance. Sturgis lay on the ground in the middle of the trail, grimacing in pain and holding his leg.

Jessie pulled up the reins, bringing her horse to a stop near the injured reporter as she drew her gun. "Where were you going in such a hurry?"

"I think I broke my leg," Sturgis moaned. "Broke it bad."

"I never heard of anyone breaking a leg good," Jessie said. Then to Ki, who was just arriving, "You ever hear of anyone breaking a leg good?"

"No," Ki answered simply.

"Damn it, woman, help me," Sturgis spat. "I'm injured!"

"Ki, what is it they do when newspapermen break their legs?" Jessie asked, turning in her saddle to face Ki.

"I heard once that they shoot them," Ki answered flatly.

"Help me you ill-tempered harlot or I'll—"

"You'll what, Mr. Sturgis?"

"Never mind, just get me to a town and a doctor," came the answer.

"I'll help you, but not before I get some answers," Jessie said, walking her horse in a slow, tight circle around Sturgis.

155

"What answers could you possibly desire at a time like this?"

"For one thing, who is that boy up the trail?"

Sturgis paused for a long time, gripping his leg tightly. "He's a boy," he said at last. "I found him outside San Francisco working as a hand."

"And Abel?"

"I don't know any Abel," Sturgis protested.

Jessie drew her Colt and fired a shot, missing Sturgis's good leg by maybe eight or nine inches. "Tell me about Abel," she demanded.

"You shot him this morning," Sturgis said. "He worked in a rodeo as a trick shooter. Ugly as sin. He did tricks, cheap little carnival tricks, until I found him."

"And they both worked for you?"

"Yes, damn you. Now, help me."

"How did it work?" Jessie asked.

"How did what work?"

As answer, Jessie fired another shot, this time between Sturgis's twisted legs.

"The boy would get into a fight, and Abel would shoot the opponent," the reporter confessed. "That was one of his side show tricks, shooting at the exact moment as another man."

"Where was he during the Bellwether Kid's shoot-outs?"

"Sometimes a roof, sometimes farther away," Sturgis said with some difficulty. "Now, for the love of everything decent, please help me."

Jessie was about to ask another question when she heard the hoofbeats. It might not have been the remaining three Denton brothers, but she wasn't about to find out. Rather, she just nodded toward Ki.

Reaching down a hand, Ki half dragged the injured newspaperman up behind him on the horse, and the three of them rode off down the trail.

By the time they reached Gatz and the girl, the horsemen were closer. Sturgis moaned in pain from the ride, but he urged Ki on just the same.

"Come on, let's get the hell out of here!" Jessie ordered as they rode up.

Gatz and the girl were already on the remaining good horse, and the five of them rode off at a full gallop. A quarter of a mile later, Jessie and Ki's horses were sucking for air. A narrow cut in the trail saved them.

For a few minutes the horses behind them stopped. Jessie supposed they'd spotted the blood and the dead horse. The animal's brand and Gatz's saddlebags would tell them they were on the right trail. When the riders began again, it was at a full gallop.

Jessie watched from just a few yards into the thick trees, partially obscured by the sloping hill as three men thundered by on the trail. They looked close enough to the Denton shot in town to be his brothers. The murderous rage in their eyes only confirmed the fact.

"We don't have much time before they realize our tracks have vanished from the trail," Ki said. "Then they will no doubt double back."

"I say we give them Sturgis," Gatz offered.

"That's right," the girl put in.

"It's a good idea, but even if they'd listen, they won't believe us, not for a second," Jessie explained.

# Chapter 18

"Then what exactly do you figure on doing?" Gatz asked.

"If all of you would just shut your mouths about a plan, then I just might be able to think of something," Jessie shot back.

"Only thing that will satisfy them is seeing Mr. Sturgis here tied over a horse, dead," Peg said.

"Shut up and let the lady think," Gatz hissed.

"Yes, by all means, you shameless sheriff's daughter, let her think," Sturgis added. Apparently the broken leg had not injured him enough to shut his mouth.

"All I said was—" Peg began, but Gatz gave her a look that could have stopped a train.

It was then that Jessie hit on the idea. The plan was so simple, it was a wonder she hadn't thought of it first thing. But then again, it was a simple idea that could get them all killed, real quick.

A half hour later they were riding out, heading toward Carson City with Jessie and Peg on one horse, Ki sharing a horse with Sturgis tied across the back like a dead man, and Gatz bringing up the rear on a third horse, also tied across it like a dead man. Both Gatz and Sturgis were covered by bedroll blankets. Gatz had a .44 Colt hidden up where his hands were supposedly tied close to his chest.

They hadn't ridden more than a few minutes before they spotted two of the Dentons riding back toward them. The two men were riding stirrup-to-stirrup on either side of the trail, both of them moving slow, looking for tracks.

As the Dentons approached, Jessie could make them out more clearly. The older, a big bearded man with a heavy gut straining against a yellow-white collarless shirt and pony-hide vest, was the first to spot them. The younger one, a slightly skinnier version without the vest or quite so big a gut, kept his eyes glued to the ground, intent on finding tracks.

Jessie raised a hand in greeting, but received no response.

When they were within a few yards, the older Denton said, "Whoa there, missy."

Jessie pulled up on the reins, bringing the horse to a stop. All five of their party were now wedged in between the two brothers. "Hello there," Jessie said.

"Now, you wouldn't be Miss Starbuck, would you?" the older outlaw brother asked.

"Matter of fact, I happen to be she," Jessie said. "But I'm afraid you have me at a disadvantage."

"Oh, I think you know who we are," the young one replied, talking for the first time.

"Your name Denton?" Jessie asked.

"This here is Ran, that's short for Randal, and they call me John, and that ain't short for nothing. You wouldn't know nothing about a newspaperfella, kinda a talky type, and this fancy-dress kid?"

"Know enough to know they're dead," Jessie said. "We were just taking what's left to Carson City."

"And we was gonna be married," Peg put in dramatically.

"That them you got tied there?" Ran asked, bringing his horse close enough to catch Jessie's bridle with one hand as he drew out a pistol with another.

"That's them," Jessie said, and watched as John Denton caught Ki's bridle in a similar fashion.

"What all happened to them?" Ran asked, suspicion rising in his voice as he eyed the bedroll containing Sturgis.

"They were partners," Jessie began. "The young one said something about the newspaperman cheating him. Got into it about five, six miles back. The young one shot the old one, then tried to shoot me. That was a mistake."

Ran Denton studied Jessie carefully, looking for some sign of lying, but finding only a cold, steady stare. "I reckon that was," he said softly. "I reckon that was his biggest mistake, outside of shooting

Kurt. But I 'spose you heard about that."

"Something, heard something about it," Jessie answered.

"Sumbitch!" Ran spat suddenly, and brought his boot out of its stirrup fast, to kick what was probably Sturgis's head.

To his credit, Sturgis didn't move.

"Them being dead and all, you wouldn't mind if I just have a see for myself, would you?" Ran asked.

Jessie shook her head. "Go on, if you got to."

"Oh, I got to," the older Denton answered. "Just to see the man dead who helped kill my baby brother."

"Me, too," John Denton offered. "I just gotta see that bastard dead."

And with that, Ran released the bridle of Jessie's horse and moved his own animal a little way forward, to lift the edge of the blanket.

Jessie held her breath as the edge of the blanket came up to reveal Sturgis in profile. The newspaperman didn't move. He didn't so much as draw a breath.

"I guess that's him, all right," came Ran's grim confirmation. "John, who they got tied there?"

The younger brother lifted the blanket concealing Gatz, taking his time to stare at the back of the young man's head. "It's him, all right," John called. "Dead as anything."

"Well, damn," Ran said. "Well, goddamn! That sumbitch!"

Jessie shrugged, as if to say, well at least they're dead and that's the important thing.

Then there was a long silence. It was the kind of silence that could have been filled with anything and could have been ended with anything. Finally Ran pulled the repeating rifle from his boot and chambered a shell. "You just don't mind if I shoot him again, do you?" he asked. "Make me feel just a whole lot better. Putting Denton lead into him would just round out my day, if you know what I'm getting at."

Jessie shrugged again, but then Sturgis stirred and spoke. "My good man, I'm certain this is all a tragic misunderstanding—" he began, but never finished. The shock of a dead man suddenly talking brought Ran's finger back on the trigger, and he shot Sturgis in the chest. Then Ran's horse came back, pawing its front hooves off the ground in fright at the shot.

John Denton reacted quickly, drawing his revolver from the holster, but before he could trigger off a shot, Gatz reared up and fired. He shot wildly, without thinking, but it was a good shot. The bullet plowed into the younger Denton, through his jaw, and exploded out the top of his head in a thick spray of blood, brain, and bone.

The dead outlaw's horse bolted forward, edging between Jessie and Ran's horses as Ran brought his gun up to get a shot at Jessie.

Ki's right hand suddenly became a blur as a *shuriken* flashed in the air. But his horse, too, was startled, and the star missed its mark, hitting Ran's claybank low on the flank and sending it into an agony of openmouthed pain and horror before it shot off, easily jumping the body of the young outlaw that lay in the center of the trail, and vanished around a bend.

Jessie had her Colt out, but couldn't bring herself to shoot a man in the back, not even an outlaw.

In less than two minutes they had Gatz untied and were galloping down the trail themselves toward Carson City. They didn't stop until the horses were in a sweat, gasping for air.

"What you gonna do now, Miss Starbuck?" Peg asked innocently.

"Way I see it, most of our worries are behind us now," she answered.

"Yes, but they may be gaining very quickly," Ki replied.

"First thing, we gotta get Sturgis buried," Jessie said, stepping down off her horse.

"Bury him? Hell, just leave him!" Gatz said. "I'm done working for him. Done and finished with it forever."

"Don't be so hasty, my young friend," Sturgis's voice spoke from under the blanket.

"Can't be," Gatz exclaimed in horror.

Jessie was already at the horse with Ki, who was cutting at the ropes with a small knife. Together they lifted Sturgis down and carried him to the side of the road while Peg gathered the horses.

"I fear, dear kind lady, that I am mortally wounded," Sturgis moaned.

Maybe he was like a snake and died in parts, Jessie thought. Maybe the tongue was just the last part to die. "You just rest easy, there," she said, examining his wound. She'd seen worse, but not on a living man.

"Miss Starbuck, kind angel, do you have a pencil?" Sturgis asked, his voice raspy.

"A what?"

"A writing implement," came the answer.

"No, nothing like that," Jessie said.

Sturgis shut his eyes slowly, and Jessie figured it was maybe for the last time. His breathing was short and ragged. The bullet, which had gone in through the chest, had probably hit something important. Maybe even a bunch of important things.

Suddenly Sturgis opened his eyes. "Then do, please, try to remember this," he said. "Try to remember it as exactly as you can. And recite it to the nearest newspaperman you meet."

Jessie nodded for an answer, not certain if the reporter saw her.

Sturgis coughed then, releasing a mouthful of bubbling, bright red blood. Then he began to talk, his voice a whispering rattle. "Byron Tyrone Sturgis, an eminent author of more than one hundred serialized true stories and countless newspaper stories, died on this date. Shot in the back by a desperate outlaw while in the pursuit of a story, the noted newspaperman will be grieved by no one but his legion of fans."

"Okay, you just rest easy now," Jessie said soothingly.

But Sturgis shook his head, coughed once more, and continued. "A favorite of society's elite, he was a welcomed guest in the finest drawing rooms of New York City, Newport, Chicago, and San Francisco. A man of great charm, wit, and personal magnetism—"

Sturgis never finished. He died in mid-sentence.

"He's dead," Jessie said, looking up at Ki, Gatz, and Peg.

"Shut his eyes," Peg said.

"Hell, shut his mouth," Gatz put in.

It took them more than an hour to cover Sturgis's body with enough rocks to keep out whatever might want to get at the carcass. Nobody even mentioned the idea of saying a few words.

"What are you planning now, Miss Starbuck?" Peg asked as they moved toward the horses.

"What I'm planning now is to get far enough up the trail so we can find a place to make camp for the night," Jessie answered. "Then, I'm planning on riding out, first thing tomorrow. You two want to follow us, you're welcome."

"Dentons sure to be in Carson City," Gatz murmured.

"We'll just think about them when we need to and not before," came the answer. "Ki and me, we've had enough. Isn't that right, Ki?"

Ki nodded slowly for an answer. It was a nod

that said he for one had had more than enough.

"Well then, I guess we'll ride with you," Peg answered, deciding for both herself and Gatz.

★

# Chapter 19

"What do you think now?" Ki asked as they rode along. For the last half mile Jessie and Ki had been inching ahead of Gatz and Peg. Now that there were twenty or so yards between them, they could talk in relative privacy.

"You heard what Sturgis told me," Jessie answered. "Said he was behind the shootings. Hired that Abel fella out of a wild west show to do the shooting for Gatz."

"And you believe it was Abel who tried to kill you and killed Dr. Seacrest?"

"Hell yes," Jessie answered quickly. "Makes sense, though, don't it? After the doctor got that telegraph, Sturgis had to do something, didn't he? So he sent Abel after us."

"Just to have something he could write about," Ki said and sighed in wonderment. "Very sad, really."

Jessie took her time in answering. "Sad or not,

I say we finish our business in Carson City and be on our way back home."

"Do you plan on telling the sheriff or marshal in Carson City? They maybe would not believe you."

"Frankly, Ki, I don't give a good damn if they believe me or not," Jessie answered, eyes fastened straight ahead. "They can do what they like with it."

"They'll want someone," Ki replied. "They may even want anyone. Maybe you'll do."

Jessie didn't have to ask what he was talking about. She already knew. With that much killing—Kurt Denton, Sturgis, Dr. Seacrest, Abel, John Denton, and Lord knew who else—the law would want to hang someone up for it. They'd want to hang a live person, the dead being bad, if not wholly unrepentant, recipients of hemp justice.

Jessie was about to say something, maybe even something about Gatz, when she heard the unmistakable click of a revolver being cocked behind her. Turning, she saw Gatz holding the Colt on her and Ki.

"Miss Starbuck, I'd be much obliged if you'd just give your gun over to Peg there," Gatz said. "And don't get no funny ideas about me not being a good shot. Maybe I ain't as handy as Abel was, but I'm good enough."

The girl spurred her horse forward, her hand already out to collect the pistol.

"What's the meaning of this?" Jessie asked, already knowing the meaning all too well.

"Meaning is, Peg and me, we've been talking," Gatz said. "Been talking and thinking, together like, and what we thought is that soon as we reach town, you're gonna go straight to the law. And I can't abide that."

Jessie handed the gun over to the girl reluctantly.

"Obliged," Peg mumbled, stuffing the gun into the waistband of her canvas pants.

"You got it all worked out, do you?" Jessie said.

"Maybe not every bitty thing," Gatz answered. "But enough, I figure. I guess I got everything figured out just enough to get by."

"That's right, darling," Peg offered in encouragement. "All we got to do is—"

"Get rid of us, is that it?" Jessie asked.

"That's about all of it," Gatz said. "I already got rid of the Bellwether Kid, didn't I?"

Gatz was right up alongside Jessie now, still holding the gun on her and Ki.

"Just tell me one thing," Jessie asked. "Why'd you go along with Sturgis for so long?"

This took a little bit of thinking, but not much, on the young man's part. "Hell, I wasn't doing nothing better," he said at last. "Seemed like a little bit of fun. And it was, for a whiles, anyway."

Jessie was about to say something else, stall for time, when a shot exploded from the trees. An instant later, Gatz was knocked from his horse.

Jessie and Ki leapt down, taking cover between the animals, as another shot exploded. One of the

170

horses, the last remaining one of Jessie's purchase, sat down hard, a bullet lodged in its side.

"Damn it to hell," Gatz moaned. "It's them Dentons again. Whyn't they just quit?"

" 'Cause you and Sturgis killed their brother," Jessie said.

"Miss Starbuck, help, he's hurt bad," Peg said, from the other side of the downed horse. "They shot him in the arm."

But Jessie and Ki were wedged between their own animals, holding the bridles for dear life, trying to stay between them as they skittered at the smell of horse blood. "Shots coming from up the hill," Ki said.

Suddenly from the hills a voice boomed out. "We just want the boy and the girl. Send them up and you can go on your way." Jessie recognized the voice as Ran Denton's.

"He's shot!" Jessie called back. "Shot bad!"

"Who'd you think shot him, lady?" Ran called back. "Now send that worthless sumbitch out!"

"Ki, can you get up there to them?" Jessie asked.

"If we move horses, then they will only shoot them," Ki said.

"We ain't gonna ask you again!" Ran shouted. "Me and my brother, we're waiting on you."

"He's bleeding," Peg said. "Bleeding bad."

Jessie squatted down. From under the horse she saw Gatz, most of his arm blown away from the shot, blood seeping out his fingers. "Tie that wound off," she said.

Another shot sounded from the trees, kicking up dust right under Jessie's horse.

"I ain't gonna abide it," Gatz said, watching as Peg tied off the wound with an old bandanna. "I ain't gonna."

"Do you have a plan, darling?" the girl asked.

"Damn right," Gatz answered, then popped his head up and fired five fast rounds with his good hand. Before the hammer fell on the last round, he was already running back toward the woods opposite the unseen gunman.

As the girl tried to follow, another shot from the hills pounded into the ground at her feet, causing her to turn and head for cover near the fallen horse. "You bastard! You rotten bastard!" she screamed as Gatz vanished into the trees. "You can't leave me here!"

Jessie turned to Ki as Gatz made good his escape. A second later another shot sounded, this one from the direction Gatz had run. It wasn't from his gun. The sound was unmistakably that of a shotgun, a big ten-gauge more than likely.

"That ends that," Jessie whispered to Ki.

"Though it has done nothing to improve our fortunes," Ki answered.

"How far do you figure it is to Carson City?" Jessie asked.

"A few miles, not far," Ki answered.

"Damn, you'd think there'd be more riders on a road like this," Jessie said.

"You would think."

"I say we start walking and see what happens," Jessie suggested.

172

"What about me?" Peg pleaded, from her cover near the dead horse. "You just can't leave me here."

For answer, Jessie pulled the reins of her and Ki's horses close and began to walk, using the animals for cover.

"You just can't leave me here," Peg moaned.

"Why not? You were going to leave us here, weren't you?"

"That was different," the girl pleaded.

Jessie pulled up on the reins, stopping the animals. "It was different. You were going to kill us first."

"Please," the girl managed.

Jessie looked at Ki, who nodded reluctantly.

"All right then, run over," Jessie said.

The girl jumped the dead horse in a single stride as a rifle bullet pounded into the dead animal's carcass. A second later she was between the two horses with Jessie and Ki.

"Where in hell you think you're going, lady?" Ran Denton shouted from his hiding place in the hills.

"Carson City," Jessie shouted back as she continued walking.

Two more shots sounded, and the horse on Ran's side fell over dead. Jessie, Ki, and Peg scrambled to get behind the other.

"What are they going to do to us?" Peg asked, her voice small and frightened.

Jessie would have answered, but Denton answered for her, shooting the other horse three times. The shots weren't clean, they hit the horse low, below the heart. The animal reared up, then spun, running forward for five yards before collapsing.

Before the last horse died, the three of them had made the trees, running furiously before arriving at a deep gulch. It was maybe fifty feet to the bottom and almost straight down. And with no handholds at all.

"We split up," Jessie said.

Ki nodded in agreement. All three of them together were an easy target.

"What did you do with my gun?" Jessie asked, turning to Peg.

The girl's hands flew to the front of her pants, but the gun was gone. "I . . . I must have lost it back there, by the horses," she said and sniffled.

"Let's go, then," Jessie said. "Ki, you go south, I'll go north."

"What about me?" Peg asked, trembling with terror.

"You can go anywhere you want," Jessie said, already on the move.

A moment later the girl was left alone as Jessie and Ki vanished into the trees. She stood there for a long time, paralyzed with fear. Then, slowly, she began walking, back out to the road. She hadn't gone twenty paces before a large man with a shotgun stepped out from behind a pine.

"Howdy there," the man said, moving the shotgun up so it was aimed at her face.

"Please, don't . . . ," Peg managed.

"Don't what?" the man said. Then, without turning, he called, "Ran, I got the girl!"

"Don't hurt me," Peg mumbled, a large tear coming down her cheek. "He made me do it."

"Do what?" the man asked, smiling.

"Everything, he made me do everything," Peg stammered.

The answer brought a smile to the man's face. "I reckon I can make it so you don't do nothing, never. I lost kin on account of you people."

"Please . . . ," Peg began. Then she started to cry as the man put the shotgun to his shoulder, his finger curling around the trigger.

As the girl closed her eyes, preparing to die, she saw a flash that snapped her eyes open.

The big man turned as the throwing star sliced through his cheek and lodged in his tongue, nearly severing it.

As a reflex brought the shotgun down and around, the girl leapt toward it. A second *shuriken* sailed through the air, lodging in the man's neck as she grabbed the gun down low on the barrel. As the gun went off, the man fell back, sending a load of double-aught buckshot into the girl's foot.

Jessie ran from her hiding place in the trees, grabbed the gun, and dispatched the man with a swift kick to the head that broke his neck with a sharp crack.

"Oh, he shot me," the girl moaned as Jessie turned back to her. Her foot was a bloody mess, but fortunately she hadn't taken anywhere near the full load. Most of the shot had pounded harmlessly into the ground between her and the gunman.

A moment later Ki was at Jessie's side.

"She's hurt," Jessie said, handing the shotgun to Ki as she knelt to the girl. Even a quick look told her that the girl would lose some toes.

Stripping her belt off, Jessie tied it around the girl's calf to stop the bleeding.

"Oh, it hurts, hurts bad," Peg moaned. "Please help."

"We've got to get her to town," Jessie said.

"She won't need no doctor," Ran's voice suddenly spoke up from close by.

Jessie turned to see Ran Denton standing maybe twenty feet off. He was holding a repeater with one hand, finger on the trigger. "You killed the one who killed your brother," she said.

Without answering, Ran walked to his fallen brother and pulled the *shuriken* from his neck. "This don't look like it could come from but one place," he said, examining the polished star carefully. Then, turning to Ki, he said, "You happen to know how this got stuck in his neck?"

Ki didn't answer, didn't even shrug.

"Suppose you hand over that scattergun," Ran said, raising the rifle slightly as he took a tentative step toward Ki.

Ki brought the gun up, holding it parallel to the ground, as if offering it to Ran.

A slow smile spread across Ran's face, and he took another step, holding out a hand for the gun.

When he was within range, Ki spun the gun, using it like a *bo*, the ancient martial-arts fighting staff. Instantly the gun was transformed into a totally different kind of weapon, becoming a blur

176

of stained black wood and dull metal.

Ran, startled, took a step back and brought the rifle up. But it was too late. Ki struck out with his left foot, catching the gunman in the chest and sending him flying backward. Before he could bring the rifle back down, Ki struck again, this time with the butt of the shotgun, driving it into Ran's face, shattering his nose.

As the gunman fell to the ground, Ki pried the rifle away from him and tossed it behind.

★

# Chapter 20

It was full dark by the time Jessie and Ki managed to tie Ran up, build a litter for Peg, and collect what equipment they could from the dead horses.

When they finally started back on the trail, it was Ran Denton, eyes blackened from the busted nose, who pulled Peg. Jessie and Ki were burdened with their saddles, saddlebags, and bedrolls. It promised to be a long walk to Carson City.

"Ki, I'm gonna ask you a favor," Jessie said. "Next time I suggest we ride to business, you stop me, hear?"

"Yes, I would advise strongly against it," came the answer. "But tell me, what do you think will happen?"

"I figure the law will get enough of the story out of these two so they can piece it together."

Ahead of them Denton was pulling Peg, and neither of them seemed happy about what lay ahead, though the girl had been much calmer since they poured a pint of Denton's whiskey down her throat. It appeared as if she almost didn't mind losing a couple of toes.

When they were just a mile or two outside of town, the rain began. It fell in huge dollop-size drops that soaked the dusty trail to mud in minutes.

"Now, that's just fine, ain't it?" Denton complained. "Nothing worse than traveling a muddied road."

As the rain soaked them through, Jessie vowed to herself she would head straight to a hotel room when they reached town. She would talk to no one. And if anyone approached, offering kind words and a blanket, well, she just might have to shoot him.

# From the Creators of Longarm!

Featuring the beautiful Jessica Starbuck
and her loyal half-American half-
Japanese martial arts sidekick Ki.

---